In the sunlight her dark hair was streaked with auburn and gold,

yet her brows and lashes were almost black, as dark as her Greek eyes, eyes that she must have inherited from her mother.

Mark let his gaze wander down the length of her body. *I thought you'd be pretty, Alexa Cord. I expected that*, he said to himself, not daring to speak aloud, for fear she wasn't quite asleep. *I just didn't know that I would like you so damn much. That makes it very tough.*

But, tough or not, he could hardly resist the temptation of her full, sensuous lips. For a moment he felt himself leaning toward her as if to kiss them. He stopped just in time, as she opened her eyes.

"I thought you were sleeping," he said softly.

Dear Reader,

When two people fall in love, the world is suddenly new and exciting, and it's that same excitement we bring to you in Silhouette Intimate Moments. These are stories with scope and grandeur. The characters lead lives we all dream of, and everything they do reflects the wonder of being in love.

Longer and more sensuous than most romances, Silhouette Intimate Moments novels take you away from everyday life and let you share the magic of love. Adventure, glamour, drama, even suspense— these are the passwords that let you into a world where love has a power beyond the ordinary, where the best authors in the field today create stories of love and commitment that will stay with you always.

In coming months look for novels by your favorite authors: Kathleen Creighton, Heather Graham Pozzessere, Nora Roberts and Marilyn Pappano, to name just a few. And whenever you buy books, look for all the Silhouette Intimate Moments, love stories *for* today's woman *by* today's woman.

Leslie J. Wainger
Senior Editor
Silhouette Books

Anna James

The Treasure of Kavos

Silhouette Intimate Moments

Published by Silhouette Books New York

America's Publisher of Contemporary Romance

SILHOUETTE BOOKS
300 East 42nd St., New York, N.Y. 10017

ISBN: 0-373-07286-4

First Silhouette Books printing May 1989

Books by Anna James

Silhouette Intimate Moments

Silhouette Special Edition

ANNA JAMES

spends most of her time in either Atlanta, Georgia, or Los Angeles, California. She has written many different kinds of romances—from historical to contemporaries, as well as numerous Gothics. When she's not traveling or writing, she enjoys tennis, the theater, long walks on the beach and her three incompatible cats.

Prologue

Sir William, I think you had best come to the store-room.'' The clerk stood nervously at the office door.

Sir William Brevort, director of Hellenic acquisitions at the British Museum, looked up sharply. "It's there, isn't it, the Aphrodite gate?" He glanced at the index card on his desk that named the donor, Sergeant Kelsey Miller, and the section in which the gift had been stored.

"It's in 114-A," came the response, "or at least part of it is there."

Sir William looked down at the card again. "Yes," he said impatiently, "I see that a portion is missing, but there's no further notation."

"It's more than a portion, actually, sir. Hera is there, and Athena, but—"

"Good heavens, don't tell me—"

"I'm afraid so, Sir William. Aphrodite is missing."

* * *

"Yes?" The voice of the man answering the phone was smooth and cultivated.

"I have a proposition to offer."

"I'm always ready to listen," the voice responded.

"The gate I mentioned to you..."

"Go on."

"The Aphrodite portion is in Greece, on an island in the Dodecanese."

"How do you know?"

"Sir William tracked down the sergeant who made the original donation."

"The man left part of it behind?" the voice asked.

"Let's say he had no choice."

"Hmm. Sounds interesting."

"Hera and Athena are in bronze as I told you, but the Aphrodite..."

"Yes?"

"The figure is said to be gold."

"And worth a great deal, I should think," the voice responded.

"Certainly worth a trip to Greece."

Chapter 1

The May sun glittered on the blue-green waters of the harbor at Kavos. A handful of fishing boats rode at anchor on the gently undulating waves. Overhead a single seagull circled lazily and then came to rest atop a mast.

On the quay, Niko Galigrides swept the cobblestones in front of his cafe and watched as a dark-haired girl made her way toward him.

"*Yassou,* Alexa," he called out.

"*Yassou,* Niko." Alexa Cord strode hurriedly across the cobblestones, her sandaled feet noiseless, her long strides rapid. The sun glittered on the waters of the harbor and found the red highlights in Alexa's dark hair, just as it found the silvery colors in the sea.

Alexa stopped in front of the large Greek man and smiled brightly, but it was a smile that barely hid an escaping sigh. "May I post another notice in your window?"

Niko put his broom aside and folded his hands over his ample belly. "No problem." Then, puckering his lips in a little pout of concern, he asked, "Not again, Alexa?"

Alexa nodded. "Again." She took a hammer and nails from her tote bag and proceeded to tack up her hand-lettered poster. "It's hard to believe that another one of my workers has left me."

"Cristo?"

Alexa nodded once more. "He heard about a job at a new hotel on Rhodes. It pays better, of course. Besides, I think he was getting tired of working alone all day. No friends around, not a single soul to talk to except me."

Niko lowered his bulk onto a stool outside the cafe door. "This is not the problem with Cristo or any of the other young men on Kavos. They are greedy, and that is all. Never satisfied, always hungry for more— more money, more girls, more of the easy life." The pucker returned to his lips. "More of everything except hard work. That they want less of," he said sadly. "So what do they do? They leave the island in search of the good life." He shook his head. "We will soon be an island of old folks."

"You can't blame the young people," Alexa said.

"No, I do not blame them. If I were a young man, I would probably do the same. Go where the tourists scatter their money."

"Some day that will be Kavos," Alexa said determinedly. When she got no positive reaction from the cafe owner, she added, "This island is more beautiful than any other in the Dodecanese—more than Rhodes or Kos or Patmos. We should be able to attract tourists, too.''

Niko smiled fondly. ''Ah, if only our own people had as much faith as you.''

''It takes more than faith, Niko. It takes a good marketing plan and advertising, letting the world know we're here. By the way,'' she said as an afterthought, ''I'm also one of your 'own people.'''

Niko chuckled.

''Well, I'm *almost* a Kavian,'' Alexa scolded. ''My mother was born on this island, and my grandfather lived here until he died.''

''And to most of the islanders, you are still an American. They think you will grow tired of your scheme and move on.''

''And you?''

Niko shrugged. ''What can I say, Alexa? I have faith in your willpower. I only wonder if that will be enough.''

''As you say on Kavos, it's no problem, Niko. And when it comes to the islanders, I'll just have to surprise them, won't I?'' A sparkle of determination flashed in her hazel eyes.

''You've been full of surprises,'' Niko admitted, ''from the very first when you came here to take over your grandfather's house.'' Bothered by the late afternoon sun that spilled down on the cobblestoned patio but unwilling to end the conversation, Niko pulled out a handkerchief and blotted the beads of perspiration on his forehead. ''Since then, everything you've done has been a surprise.'' He chuckled to himself. "No one, not the men of Kavos certainly, expected that you could wield a hammer."

"If they could see me in action, they still wouldn't believe it," Alexa answered. "I don't have the most professional touch."

"So? The nail goes in. Nothing else matters. Now, before the sun melts us, come inside. Maria will make you a coffee."

"Another time, thanks, Niko." Alexa picked up her tote bag. "It's time to wield the hammer again and put up the rest of these signs."

"Are you going to post one of them in the butcher shop?" Niko asked.

"Anywhere I can."

Niko laughed and mopped his face again. "I bet old Yianni would like to come and help with Alexi's house. I've seen the way he watches you."

"And I've seen the way his wife watches him watching me! No, even if Yianni volunteered to work for nothing, I'd turn him down."

"What you need is a husband, Alexa," Niko said. This was an oft-repeated conversation, one that Niko never tired of.

Alexa flashed him a smile and gave her usual answer. "I'm up on the hills waiting, Niko. Send along any likely candidates, but just be sure they can use a hammer." She waved goodbye and crossed the square around which the little harbor town of Kavos was clustered.

On the harborside, next to Niko's taverna, there was a tobacco shop, a post office that also sold ferry tickets, and Yianni's butcher shop, which Alexa studiously avoided. On the other side of the street were a grocery store and a few stores with clothing, hardware and the usual souvenirs—sponges, worry beads, hand-painted plates. At nearly all of the establishments Alexa's Help Wanted notices fluttered in the breeze.

Rising up behind the harbor and the town were the green hills of Kavos that so tempted Alexa. Soon, she was sure, they would tempt the tourists, as well. She headed for them, but something stopped her as she turned onto the road that led to the village church and the sacred grotto where one of the lesser saints had been visited by the Virgin Mary, or so the local legend went.

It wasn't the sound of the ferry boat docking that made her hesitate. She'd heard that a hundred times and paid little or no attention to it unless she was waiting for supplies from Rhodes. It was more a feeling, as if someone were watching her. She turned and looked back over her shoulder. The sun was low on the horizon, almost obliterating her view of the boat as it pulled into the dock. She squinted and raised her hand to shade her eyes.

Then she saw him, a lean, determined-looking man stepping onto the quay, the setting sun shadowing his features. What made her pause she couldn't have said—certainly not his looks, since they weren't discernible. It must have been something in his stance, a kind of ownership, as if the island belonged to him. Not a chance, she said to herself. No one had a right to this island but the people of Kavos, not even Americans, and something told her that was exactly what he was. With a shrug, she turned and headed home, taking the road to her right.

It was narrow and cobblestoned and wound among the houses that hovered over the street. The sun glimmered on the whitewashed facades, blue shutters and window boxes filled with red geraniums, turning them into storybook pictures. She stepped back into a doorway as an old man came down the hill, leading a donkey laden with kindling, looking just like another picture from a storybook.

It was Vassili on his way to market. As he passed, the old man touched the tip of his dark blue, narrow-brimmed cap and continued on his way. But that was only a ruse, a little game he played. Vassili couldn't possibly pass by a friend without stopping for conversation. And Alexa was a friend, at first by virtue of the fact that she was Alexi's granddaughter, later because he approved of her.

As soon as Vassili reached an opening between the houses where there was room for two people and a donkey to stand together, he maneuvered the animal around, released the halter and greeted Alexa more effusively. "How does it go with you?" he asked.

"Well," Alexa responded. "But it will be even better when I find another worker."

"You are on your own again?" They spoke in Greek—his rapid, Alexa's more halting.

"They are lazy, these young men," he said, echoing Niko. "If only I were young again!" They both laughed as he assured her, "The fates will find someone for you, do not worry, Alexa. Are you on the way home now?"

"After I stop for a few minutes to visit with my Aunt Sophie."

"Then I will let you go along. Give Sophie my best," he said, tipping his hat again before giving his mule a gentle prod in the ribs. "*Herete,* Alexa."

"*Herete,* Vassili."

Alexa turned down the alleyway and at the next row of houses knocked on her great-aunt Sophie's whitewashed door. She was immediately greeted and ushered inside.

"Come and have some sweet vermouth with me." At the expression on her niece's face, Sophie laughed. "Or perhaps retsina. I know you prefer it." Sophie was a striking woman, tall and stately, not overweight but full-figured. She had a large patrician nose, dark hair streaked with gray and high cheekbones. It was easy to see where Alexa got her exotic good looks.

Alexa made herself comfortable in the living room, which was dotted with family photographs. Sophie Pappas was her father's youngest sister. Her husband had been dead for years, and her children were scattered from Athens to Australia. She visited them all frequently but declined their offers to stay. Kavos was her home, and she was happy there.

After a sip or two of the tart retsina wine, Alexa admitted, "I've been putting notices in the village again for another helper. I doubt if there's anyone left on the island to apply."

"You have had bad luck," Sophie said.

"If only I'd known," Alexa responded gloomily, sinking lower in her chair until she was resting on her spine.

"Regretting your move here?" Sophie sat ramrod straight, causing Alexa to correct her own posture and try to match her aunt's cheerful expression.

"No," she said quickly and then went on. "I don't think so." After a moment she added, "I am pleased that Pappous left his home to me."

Sophie laughed. "I'm sure your sisters were just as pleased at their grandfather's gesture. It gave them a small cash inheritance and a few pieces of jewelry while you were saddled with an old house in the Aegean."

"A wonderful old house," Alexa corrected her aunt, her mood brightening with her return to upright posture. "It just needs a little work."

At that the two women looked at each other and burst into laughter.

"Oh, Sophie," Alexa said at last, "can I ever turn that barn into a hotel?"

"I think you can. The question is, how do you feel about it? Do you still have faith in yourself?"

Alexa didn't have to think about that. "Yes," she said staunchly, "I believe in myself."

"And I believe in you also."

"Well, that makes two of us. My parents certainly don't, and neither do my two overachieving sisters."

"It's never easy being the youngest," Sophie said sympathetically.

"Especially if one sister is happily married to a doctor and has two perfect children and a great career in real estate, and the other sister is about to graduate first in her class from Yale law school."

"You're just a late bloomer," Sophie said reassuringly.

Alexa thought about that on her way up the hill to her grandfather's house. She had never actually felt inferior to her sisters, just different. Their lives didn't really seem so wonderful to Alexa. On the other hand, her life suited her fine. She was happy doing just what she wanted, and if it didn't work out, no one could ever say it was for lack of trying.

Besides, she had the greatest view on Kavos and maybe in the world. Stopping to turn around at the top of the hill near her grandfather's house, Alexa gazed down on the village and the harbor beyond.

Then she went inside, leaving the view and confronting reality. She went to the cupboard, tore off a piece of bread, cut a slice of goat cheese and made a sandwich. That would be her dinner. One of the rude awakenings she'd had when she'd arrived in Greece to lay claim to the house was its lack of a refrigerator. There was an old icebox that was too large for her to keep filled with ice. All part of the reality.

There were other parts, many of them. The stove was wood burning, and she still hadn't learned to use it correctly. The electricity was iffy at best, but at least it existed—which was more than she could say for the houses on the other side of the hill. Electricity had never gotten that far. She also had running water, but at the moment the heater was on the blink, so it was cold water only.

The house was a relic—that was about the best way to describe it. Few of the windows opened. Those that did had to be propped up, and several panes were broken. The floors sagged, and the whole place seemed to moan and creak with old age. And she loved it. Someday she would share the house and its surrounding beauty with a deluge of guests—if she ever found a carpenter to help her get it into shape.

At the rate Alexa was going, it would never be opened for the tourist season in June. On the other hand, there didn't seem to be any tourists on Kavos, anyway. That was the major rude awakening she was going to have to face. Or do something about.

Alexa took her sandwich and nibbled at it as she moved back through the house and out to the garden. There were fine beaches rimming the shore of Kavos, which would be appealing to the tourists who arrived in Greece every summer looking for sunshine and sea.

But there were no ruins to speak of, at least not by Greek standards, except for the lovely temple to Apollo on the other side of the island. It was quite respectable and worth investigating, if only the tourists could find it. Or find the island for that matter. With no airport and a ferry that called only three times a week if tourists were lucky, Kavos might just stay hidden forever.

"Not if I can help it," Alexa said aloud as she brushed off a section of the stone wall and sat down beside the garden, trying to ignore how much work needed to be done there. She just hadn't had time for weeding and transplanting. There were more urgent problems to face first.

Looking down the hill, with the sun glinting in the distance and the leaves of the olive trees stirring softly in the afternoon breeze, revealing their silvery undersides, Alexa thought again that there was no more beautiful place in the world. Even though it seemed as if she'd never reach her goal of opening a hotel on Kavos, at times like this she knew she wouldn't give up. Somehow she'd make it work.

A fence with a rickety wooden gate surrounded the house. It was picturesque if nothing else, and Alexa had been reluctant to tear it down. There was a brass knocker on the gate, but no one had ever used it. Every visitor just came right in because the iron latch had rusted long ago.

But today the sound of someone knocking on it finally permeated her daydreams. She got up and crossed the garden quickly, curious to find out what stranger had made the trek up the mountain.

He wasn't really a stranger, at least not in the strictest sense of the word. She'd seen him before in the distance. Up close, he was not quite such a romantic figure as he'd been earlier when he'd stepped off the boat with the sun behind him, creating an intriguing silhouette. He was tall with blond hair badly in need of a trim and a couple of day's growth of beard. He was wearing jeans, a blue denim shirt and a pair of once-white sneakers. In his hand was one of her Help Wanted notices.

"Hello," Alexa said. "Can I help you?"

"You must be Alexa," he said in a voice that was decidedly British. That surprised her, for some reason she'd expected him to be an American. "I saw this flier in one of the stores and thought I'd take a chance that you hadn't hired anyone yet."

There was something appealing about him, but something else told her that he didn't have the slightest clue about being a handyman.

"Yes, I'm Alexa." Thinking that she might as well give him a chance to prove her wrong, Alexa stepped aside and let him in to the garden.

"My name is Mark Everett," he said, extending his hand. "I just hopped off the ferry a little while ago and saw your notice in the—well, it's all over town," he continued with a grin. "The owner of the taverna gave me directions to your house." His eyes swept across the hills toward the sea. "You have a great view."

"Yes," she agreed. "I don't think it can be equaled anywhere in the Dodecanese." Alexa stopped herself, wondering why she was touting the view and wondering, too, what Niko had been thinking to send her an applicant who could have been an escapee from the sixties with his backpack and the beginnings of a beard. He looked more like a hippie than a carpenter.

"Did Niko explain what I'm looking for?" she asked, getting right down to business and expecting that she would be dismissing him quickly. "I need a combination carpenter, plumber, electrician and miracle worker to help me get this house in shape. Maybe I'm exaggerating a little when I say miracle worker, but there's so much to do that I can't imagine hiring anyone at this point who isn't skilled in all the areas I've mentioned."

"What do you think your chances are of finding that kind of superman here in Kavos?" he asked pointedly.

"Probably nil," she admitted, a little peeved that he was so quick to point out the impossibility of her task. It really wasn't his place to make that kind of judgment unless he was a superman himself, which she doubted very seriously.

He wasn't paying any attention to her reaction, but instead was looking up at the two-story house that loomed beside them. "It's a big place for one person. Or maybe you have family joining you?"

"No, I'm here alone." Her mother would have been aghast at Alexa's confiding such a thing to a complete stranger, but very little about her was a secret on Kavos. She decided to fill him in, just in case Niko hadn't done so. "I inherited this place from my grandfather. My plan," she added, trying to sound confident, "is to turn it into a pension. You know, a kind of bed and breakfast place."

"It's a fine location," Mark said as he took off his dark glasses and hooked them on his pocket. She couldn't help noticing his thick, dark lashes and incredibly blue eyes that were exactly the color of the Greek sky. Neither of which had anything to do with his expertise in plumbing, Alexa told herself.

"There's an awful lot of work to be done," she said, trying to focus again on his qualifications, which she was fairly certain were limited. "Have you had much experience with remodeling?"

"A little," he answered evasively as he moved toward the house and pulled out a penknife. Chipping away at a window, he said, "Looks like you have rotting wood here. The window probably needs to be reframed."

"Yes, I know," Alexa said. In fact, she hadn't noticed that particular problem, and inwardly she winced. More work, more expense. "Exactly what are your qualifications, Mr.—"

"Mark," he corrected with a smile. "Everything and nothing, I guess. Jack of all trades, master of none."

"I'm sorry," Alexa said, telling herself that it was ridiculous even to be talking to this man, a perfect stranger, a drifter whom she shouldn't even have let in the gate, blue eyes or not. "I really need someone with specific skills. As you can see—"

"I majored in ancient Greek at Cambridge," he said, flashing that smile again.

"Mark, I'm sorry, really." Alexa decided to stop the conversation before it went any further. His British education, if there had been such a thing, didn't interest her in the least.

But he was persistent. "I taught for a while," he continued, "did some translations, lived hand to mouth, and when I realized there was a limited need for Greek scholars, I worked on a construction crew. I really have done something of everything—building, plumbing, electrical work."

Even though the story he told wasn't so different from her own, Alexa wasn't taken in. Mark Everett looked less like a carpenter than anyone she'd ever seen. "Listen, Mark, I appreciate your applying, but I don't think you'd be right for this job."

"What do you have in mind, a sturdy Greek type born with a wrench in his hand?" He dropped his knapsack, put his hands in his pockets and looked down at her with his challenging blue eyes. "How much luck have you had with them?"

Obviously he'd been talking to Niko. "I'll admit the ones with talent don't last long. In fact, the ones without talent don't last much longer," she added. "Are you planning to stay on Kavos for a while?" The question was her undoing—he knew she'd weakened.

"For a while. I saved up enough for passage, but I'm running low on funds, and I came over to Kavos from Rhodes since I heard it was cheaper to live here."

"Cheaper and quieter. There isn't much going on." Alexa felt compelled to warn him of all the pitfalls. She didn't want to commit herself only to be left without a helper again when he got bored and moved on.

"That's fine. I'm working on a translation of Thucydides, and I could use some peace and quiet. Carpentry during the day and translating at night. It could be beneficial for both of us."

"I don't suppose you have any letters of recommendation."

"Not a one," he answered with a grin. "But I can quote Sophocles."

Alexa tried to dismiss his intellectual side. It had nothing to do with wiring and roofing, but she was wavering and she knew it.

"Listen, Alexa, I have an idea. Give me a task. A labor, like Hercules in the myths. If I pass, then you'll hire me, if I can't handle it, then I'll pack up my knapsack and hit the road again."

Alexa took a deep breath. That seemed reasonable enough, and at this point she didn't have anything to lose. No one else had applied. If he really could do the job, she'd be a fool to turn him away.

"Well," she said slowly. "I've been having a problem with a stopped-up kitchen sink. I've tried everything, to no avail."

"Do you have a wrench?"

"Of course," she replied. "I have every tool available on Kavos."

He followed her into the kitchen, and Alexa saw his eyes quickly take it all in—the old stove, the icebox, the wooden table she'd repainted, the cold stone floor. "A little primitive," she said apologetically.

"But very charming," he answered, which pleased her enormously. It was the charm that had appealed to her in the first place and that she hoped to keep when the remodeling was complete. "Now, let's get to the problem," he said, jarring her back to reality.

The sink was a big, white, galvanized monstrosity. After looking down into the cavernous hole covered by an inch of water that adamantly refused to drain, Mark turned on the taps and waited. The water sputtered out, adding to the accumulation already in the sink. He put his hand under the flow. "Ice cold," he said. "Surely you have a hot-water heater."

"The flame went out," Alexa admitted.

"Easily fixed," he said with confidence. "But this is another matter." He dropped down, resting on his haunches to look under the sink. "You'll probably need to replace all these pipes eventually, but they look okay for now. Bring me your toolbox," he commanded, and Alexa found herself complying, his self-assured tone lifting her spirits.

Mark opened the toolbox, scanned the contents, chose a wrench and ducked back under the sink. "I'll need a bucket, too," he called out.

Alexa fetched the bucket and shoved it under the sink, but not without a comment. "If I do decide to hire you, Mark Everett, that doesn't mean I'll be your helper. Just remember, it's the other way around." Something told her she needed to make that clear.

For a while Mark worked silently with the wrench, but as the pipe joint began to loosen, she saw his arm relax and waited for his response. It came quickly. "If I go to work for you, Alexa Cord, I'll learn where everything is kept and fetch it for myself."

With that he went back to work. He'd pushed his sleeves up, and Alexa was surprised to see that his arms were tanned and muscular. He wasn't the lanky, bookish man he'd seemed to be on first glance. Well, muscles didn't make a plumber. But at this moment they seemed to help.

After one slip with the wrench that caused him to swear softly, Mark managed to remove the U-joint. Water from the pipe gushed into the bucket, and Alexa breathed a sigh of relief.

"What was the problem?" she asked.

"It's hard to say. These old pipes are so rusty that almost anything can catch in them and cause a backup. Something as small as an olive pit. You'll just have to be careful until you have them replaced."

"That'll be a long time down the road," Alexa said, thinking of all the essential work that had to be done first.

"Well, we're definitely going to have to replace this section," Mark said after he retightened the connection and struggled to his feet.

"We?" Alexa asked.

"I guess I'm jumping to conclusions." Mark rolled his sleeves back down and glanced at Alexa with just the hint of a grin. He knew he had her.

Even though he wasn't the most adept plumber she'd ever seen, he was pretty good for an amateur. The water was flowing again. He'd already turned it on and leaned over to take a long drink from the spigot.

"I do have glasses," she said.

"Not necessary. This water is so cold and fresh it must come from a spring."

"Yes," she told him. "The source is way up in the hills. It forms a stream that flows down into my cistern. I doubt if there's purer water anywhere in the world."

Mark straightened up, wiped his mouth with the back of his hand and grinned again. He was clearly waiting for her decision.

"All right," Alexa said, remembering that he'd also noticed the rotten window frames, which was more than any of her other so-called experts had done. "We'll give it a try. Maybe a week."

"Make it two," he suggested. "Enough time for me to get acclimated."

"Two weeks then, but first I need to tell you that my wages aren't comparable with the States or England." She named her hourly rate, but he was already laughing.

"I hadn't expected to be paid on a scale with U.S. plumbers," he said, holding out his hand to seal the bargain. "Your pay will be enough for a place in town." He paused, waiting for her to shake his hand, which she finally did. "Unless room and board is thrown in as part of my salary. This is a big house."

He was still holding her fingers as his blue eyes laughed into hers. He'd worked up a sweat, and Alexa noticed that his hair was curling around his forehead. She withdrew her hand, aware that he was flirting with her and that she'd almost flirted back. Almost, but not quite.

"Not big enough," she answered a little vaguely. "I suggest you ask Niko for his ideas about a good rooming house. Meanwhile I'll see you at eight in the morning. Life starts early here on Kavos."

That was about as businesslike a command as she could muster, and Alexa had a feeling that it didn't sound as formal as she'd hoped. He was still grinning when he picked up his knapsack, gave a mock salute and headed for the door. "See you at eight."

As he adjusted the straps of his pack over his shoulders and set off down the path toward town, Mark couldn't help whistling. Everything had gone well. Alexa had been suspicious at first and definitely not eager to hire a drifter, even one with credentials in Greek history. His offering to undergo a test had been a spur-of-the-moment idea and one hell of a bluff. Fortunately she'd chosen something he could do. God knows he'd spent enough time over the years in flats with plumbing problems—stopped-up drains not the least of them.

But he was certainly no electrician, and Mark had a feeling the house was beset with electrical problems. He thought about the books in his knapsack. Along with the Thucydides was a copy of something called, in no uncertain terms, *Everything You Ever Needed to Know About Remodeling*.

Well, there was a great deal Mark needed to know, but he'd always followed instructions fairly easily. He could handle it.

He wasn't so sure he could handle Alexa, though. Mark had been prepared for her good looks, dark shining hair and interesting eyes that were a mixture of brown and green and gold, skin that was a sunny color not quite olive and not quite cream, another mixture that blended Greek and American.

He'd been prepared for all of that. He remembered seeing her as he stepped off the boat, a lithe figure gliding across the cobblestones. The sun had caught in that glorious hair, and she'd turned and looked at him, or so Mark thought. He still couldn't be sure. But he'd seen her all right, in an unforgettable moment. Yes, he'd been prepared for her beauty.

What he hadn't been prepared for was her independence. He'd expected her to be more vulnerable, more anxious for someone to come along and offer help, but she hadn't given in so easily. She'd known what she wanted, and he hadn't been sure until the last moment that he would qualify.

Now that he had, Mark was determined to become indispensable to Alexa, always there for her, helping in whatever way he could. And if he ran into trouble with repairs, he'd manage to work them out somehow. He had a contact in Athens who could probably talk him through just about any problem. Alexa would get the help she needed so desperately, and the job wouldn't be a hardship to him.

Quite the contrary. Now that he was back in his beloved Greece, working each day in the sun with the Aegean only a glance away, there wouldn't be any complaints. He had four weeks maximum, and somehow Mark had the feeling that this time was going to be very special. This time he was going to enjoy every moment.

Chapter 2

Alexa stood atop a ladder, struggling to hold the sign steady with one hand while she tried to hammer in a tack with the other, a task that was rapidly proving to be beyond her skill. Not about to be defeated by something so inconsequential, she tried again, barely missing her thumb with the hammer.

"*Kalimera,* Alexa," a voice called out. "Good morning. Need a hand?"

She glanced down to see Mark standing at the foot of the ladder. It was 8:00 a.m. exactly. He was prompt if nothing else. "Yes," she admitted. "I'm afraid I lack a certain skill."

"Climb down," he advised, and Alexa carefully did as she was told. Ladders, like hammers, were among her least favorite objects. She was definitely going to have to learn how to get along with all the fix-up paraphernalia.

When she reached solid ground beside him, Mark immediately climbed up and posted the sign high above the gate. "Villa Alexi, eh?" he called. "Does this mean all I had to do was fix the drain and your inn is open?" With a quick jump he was beside her, eyes laughing as usual.

Alexa shook her head. "The sign's not for the public, at least not yet. It's there as an inspiration for me, to give me extra courage, fortitude and . . ."

"Gumption?" he suggested. "Spirit?"

"Expertise," she added with a laugh. "If such a thing can be gained just through wanting it."

"I'm sure it can if you want it badly enough," he said, returning the hammer to her.

Looking up at him, Alexa noticed that he appeared quite different today. He'd shaved off the few days' growth of beard and seemed even more like a scholar and less like a carpenter. She hoped that looks didn't mean anything in Mark's case, but she didn't fail to let him know she appreciated the effort. "You look quite presentable clean-shaven," she said, and then wondered if her words sounded slightly condescending. If so, he didn't seem to notice.

"I decided it was time for a new image to go with my new life as a carpenter."

"This is just a trial period, remember," Alexa warned.

"I realize that, but I also believe that you'll be more than satisfied with me. With my work," he corrected himself without even the hint of a smile. He was leaning against the gate, holding it closed so that Alexa couldn't get by. Unless she wanted to make a scene, she had no choice but to wait until he got around to moving aside so they could go in, but she was having difficulty waiting under the intense gaze he'd turned on her.

Finally Alexa responded to his remark. "That remains to be seen, doesn't it? If you'll come inside, we can go over the work that needs to be done. I've made a list of projects."

Mark opened the gate and let her lead the way through the garden into the house. "I'm sure you have," he said as he followed her.

Alexa turned to look at him, but his face was expressionless.

"My list is in the kitchen."

"I'm right behind you," he answered.

This time she didn't bother to turn around and check out his expression but walked through into the kitchen, picked up a pad from the table and handed it to him.

"As you can see, it's a long list. I've repainted this room and ordered a new refrigerator. It's coming by ferry from Rhodes. I can live with the stove as soon as I learn to master it."

"It's a great old relic," he said. "I remember one just like it."

"Really? I wouldn't have thought such an antiquated object could be found anywhere else."

"There're all sorts of surprises in this so-called modern world," he reminded her. "Besides, where I was living at the time could hardly be called modern."

Alexa was getting curious. Surely Oxford had up-to-date appliances. "Oh, where was that?"

"A country far away. And long ago," he added. "Now what about the rest of this room?" He was definitely not interested in continuing the conversation, and Alexa was almost relieved. She really hadn't meant to get personal.

"Well, the sink is all right now that you've fixed it."

"It was nothing," he said with a little bow, "but don't forget that we're going to have to replace a couple of fittings. In the meantime, I'll get to the hot-water heater today."

"Great," Alexa said. "Cold showers are beginning to lose their attraction for me." She motioned for Mark to follow her through an alcove into the next room. It was a large, airy space with a high, beamed ceiling. "Perfect for dining," Alexa said. "In the storage room, there's an old extension table I'm planning to refinish. It'll seat twelve people, and out here through these doors I want to put breakfast tables."

"They'll be nice by the garden," he told her as they stepped out onto the cobblestoned patio.

"Well, the so-called garden is more a home to the weeds at the moment, but as soon as I get time..." Her voice trailed off, but Mark really hadn't been listening, anyway.

He'd been watching her, an occupation he could easily get used to, especially today when she looked so cool and fresh. She didn't seem to be wearing any makeup, which might have been why she looked especially young. Or it could have been the morning light. Or maybe he was just looking at her carefully for the first time, although it seemed like he'd done nothing but look at her from the moment they'd met.

She was wearing shorts and a T-shirt that was too big but still managed to show off her figure, and it was definitely a figure worth showing off. A little reluctantly, Mark forced himself to listen as he followed her through the living room, which was dominated by a tiled fireplace, then down a narrow hallway to an open door. "This is my room," she told him, and he immediately regained his interest. "You can see the effect I've achieved here. It's basically what I want for the other rooms."

He took it all in—the simple iron bed, the blue and white coverlet, the wooden chest of drawers and straight-backed chair. There was also a table that she seemed to be using for her desk. It was piled high with paperwork. Other than a framed picture on the table, there was nothing personal in the room. Mark felt suddenly disappointed, as if he'd been robbed of a chance to get close to her.

"Apparently you're going for the monastic look," he said.

Alexa was unperturbed. "I guess you can call it that. It's elegant and restful. Or at least that's what I've tried to achieve. Guests will come to Villa Alexi for the simple but classic things in life."

"Is that why you came to Greece, for the simple life?"

"I guess it's one of the reasons," she said. Mark could tell that she'd considered the question carefully, and yet she was quick to move on to what was at hand. "Now, the adjoining bath is a real problem. You might want to begin here and do something...well, I was going to say spectacular, but I guess that's the wrong word for a bathroom."

"Maybe not," he responded. "So what were the others?"

"Other what?"

"Other reasons you came to Greece, to Kavos."

She frowned slightly, and it was obvious that she didn't want to get caught up in the conversation. Yet, it was equally obvious that she had a very strong answer for his question. "To get away on my own and prove myself."

"By running an inn?"

"Yes, I guess so. I'd always wanted to do just that, and my grandfather's will made it possible. Now, about this bathroom..."

"Spectacular is definitely the wrong word," he said, agreeing with her earlier assessment. He'd glanced quickly around the room and decided it left everything to be desired. It was big, with warped wooden floors and a great deal of wasted space. The fixtures were hopeless.

"I'd construct a walk-in closet. This is the perfect place for one to use up all the wasted space. Then I'd dump the fixtures and start all over."

"Very expensive ideas," she said.

"Alexa, you asked for my evaluation, and I'm giving it." Mark paused long enough to consider how nice her name sounded on his lips. He didn't remember having spoken it before, at least not consciously. Quickly he got back to the subject at hand, which he managed to veer away from often during the morning. "You can keep the tub. It's galvanized and weighs about two thousand pounds. Not the greatest-looking thing in the world, but they don't make them like that anymore, and it won't give you any problems. But the lavatory and toilet have to go. As for the floor, surely tile is cheap here on Kavos.''

"Do you know how to lay tile?'' she questioned.

"I'll learn,'' he answered firmly. "How difficult can it be? Now, can you afford new fixtures?''

"Not really, but I've already bought them.''

"What?''

"At least the sink and toilet. They're in the storage room,'' she explained.

"So much for your remark about my expensive ideas.''

"I just wanted to make sure we were on the same wavelength,'' Alexa explained.

"And are we?''

"I think so,'' she admitted.

"Then I guess it's time for me to begin.''

She smiled. "Sounds good to me.''

The smile was followed by an awkward moment while they stood looking at each other.

Alexa started to glance away and then was drawn back to him. She wished that he would say something and release her from this embarrassing moment, but he didn't seem to have any inclination to do so, and for some reason she was speechless.

Finally she found her voice. "Maybe you should start here in the bathroom.''

For a brief moment he didn't answer, and just when she was getting ready to repeat the sentence he spoke up, sounding completely natural, as if the long pause hadn't even occurred. "You got it, boss. Just show me where you've hidden the appliances.''

Several hours later, Alexa called out from the garden, "Mark, would you like some lunch?''

He stepped outside and squinted in the sun. He'd taken off his shirt, and his long, lean body glistened with a light sheen of perspiration. The muscles she'd noticed in his arms when he'd been working on the sink had surprised her at the time. Now she was aware that his chest and shoulders were unusually broad for his long frame and more muscular than she had expected. She was less surprised by that than fascinated.

She watched as he pulled on his T-shirt and answered from somewhere inside of it, his voice muted, "Thanks, Alexa. I'm really hungry. Guess I should have brought something."

"It's only a sandwich," she said. "I thought we'd eat outside." She was beginning to feel a little silly, as if she'd spent time making plans for lunch with her brand-new worker, which she really hadn't. "I have some beer, but it's not very cold." Somehow that made her feel better. It really would have been embarrassing for everything to be perfect.

He just nodded, took the sandwich and beer and settled on the grass beneath a tree, his long legs crossed at the ankles.

Alexa sat beside him. The scent of the garden seemed to envelop them. In spite of its overgrown condition, the spring flowers had managed to emerge from the undergrowth with their fragrance intact.

Mark took a big bite of his sandwich and exclaimed, "This is great, Alexa."

"I'm fairly outstanding when it comes to sandwiches, but put me in a real kitchen setting and I fail abysmally. When the inn opens, I'll have to hire a good chef."

Mark took a long swig of his beer and propped the bottle up in the grass. "I'm not so much worried about the inn opening as I am about the guests you expect to flock into it. Just one day was enough to give me an idea that this isn't exactly a tourist mecca."

"I'm aware of that," Alexa answered defensively. Then, realizing that the island's economy was hardly Mark's fault, she added, "A little judicious marketing campaign, some well-placed advertising coupled with word-of-mouth publicity, and I think we can get things going. After the first wave of people get a whiff of this island paradise, we won't be able to keep the tourists away."

"I guess you know about such things," Mark said, readily admitting his lack of expertise. "Have you managed an inn before?"

"No, but I worked in one for several summers. It was on a little island off the coast of Maine. I was very happy there," she said pensively. "It reminds me just a little of Kavos with the rocks and the evergreen trees."

Mark was very quiet. He leaned back against the tree, finished his sandwich and beer and just listened.

Alexa smiled in remembrance. "The couple who owned that island inn seemed so complete, so self-sufficient. It was their home *and* their livelihood. I always thought that was the perfect life." For a moment she was silent, and for that same moment, Mark was afraid that she wasn't going to tell him any more about herself. Then she continued.

"The air was much more invigorating in Maine, the sunshine more penetrating, the scents more vivid and even the people more—'' She started to laugh. "I sound like the chamber of commerce, don't I?''

"The what?"

"Chamber of commerce. Oh, that's right,'' she said, remembering that he was English. "Another phrase for the mouthpiece of whatever spot needs some hype. We could use a chamber of commerce right here on Kavos. Anyway,'' she added, "those summers were the happiest of my life. I never thought I'd have the chance to duplicate them.''

Mark almost didn't want to respond, but he felt he had to warn her, even though there was nothing in his plan that made it necessary to do so. Quite the contrary, in fact. "You might have an uphill battle, Alexa.''

"I know. I've heard all the negatives. My family has cornered the market on dire predictions.''

Mark realized that while he was pointing out truisms, she was not altogether willing to see them clearly. In fact, she was getting defensive, probably because of her parents' attitude.

"Families are like that,'' he said finally.

"Mine probably had good reason,'' she admitted. "I've been through lots of jobs, never had any that I cared about, and while I was always happy enough floating around from one place to another, my father probably hit the nail on the head when he said I had definite dilettante inclinations. I never even envied my high-achieving sisters.''

Mark smiled, closed his eyes and then opened them again to swat at a bee. "My father had similar ideas. When I began my studies in ancient Greek, he frequently reminded me that there wasn't any money in it.''

"There're other rewards," Alexa said adamantly.

"We hope," Mark answered with a smile. "But whatever the rewards, you certainly were gutsy to come here alone."

"Ignorance is bliss. My grandfather loved this house. I could have sold it, but somehow I realized that when he left it to me, he did so for a reason. I guess he knew what a pushover I am for beautiful old places, no matter what their condition. Besides, I've always had strong feeling for family. I didn't want this house to fall into a stranger's hands." Alexa was beginning to relax, enjoying this time with Mark, enjoying his interest in what was so important to her.

"Did you visit here as a child?" he asked.

"One summer when I was ten years old. I'll never forget the wonderful stories he told. I guess I was the best listener of all the kids. I was fascinated by the secrets of this old house."

"Secrets?" Mark's voice held a lazy kind of disinterest. "Like buried treasure, that sort of thing?"

Alexa shook her head. "Maybe that's what he wanted me to think. I never was quite sure. Now I am. He was talking about other kinds of secrets, the treasure of a good life, the hidden clue to happiness." She was thoughtful for a moment. "Of course, he often colored his tales with the lives of the gods and goddesses, Zeus, Aphrodite, Apollo."

"A true Greek," Mark added with a laugh. "He must have been very special to you."

"I loved him unequivocally. He was quite a man, born and brought up on this island, in this house."

Mark was just about to ask another question when a voice from the other side of the stone wall interrupted them. "*Yassou,* Alexa."

"That can only be Vassili," Alexa said. "Speaking of stories, he has a stockpile unequalled in the Greek islands. Come on," she said as she got to her feet. "I'm sure you'll enjoy meeting him."

Mark wasn't at all sure. He could easily have whiled away the afternoon listening to Alexa. Now he was going to have to listen to some old Greek philosophize, for he had long ago decided that's what they all did, rich or poor, ignorant or well educated. Every Greek was a philosopher.

Mark waited as Alexa ran to the gate to let the old man in. He could hear their voices of greeting, hear Alexa's careful Greek. He was a little surprised at her pronunciation, which was quite good for an American speaking a language as difficult as Greek. The girl did have determination—she'd learned the language and learned it well.

As the voices grew closer, it was apparent that Mark had been right, the old man was a talker.

"I brought you fish for dinner," he heard Vassili declare. "My son caught it this morning."

"Thanks, Vassili," Alexa answered, responding with an invitation that made Mark sigh audibly. "Will you come in and have some coffee?"

"Yes, coffee would be nice," the old man said.

"Then come into the kitchen while I make it for you. But first you'll have to start a fire in the stove unless you want to wait around while I do it. I'm still very inept."

"I'll do it for you," Mark interjected as he stepped into the room to join them.

Quickly and, Mark thought, with a little embarrassment, Alexa introduced the two men. Vassili looked Mark over without warmth but with a great deal of curiosity, speaking in rapid Greek which Mark answered in kind. That didn't go over well. Obviously the old man had expected a foreigner with a foreigner's ways. That Mark spoke the language didn't seem to soften him in the least.

Vassili hurried to start the fire, and Mark wasn't about to challenge him. It was ridiculous, he thought, to be competing for Alexa, a woman he hardly knew, with this old man.

As Alexa assembled the coffee-making supplies, she reminded Vassili, "I'm not an expert at this yet, either, but I'm working on it." Then she turned to Mark. "Would you like some coffee?"

He nodded wordlessly and watched as she went about the involved preparations for making Greek coffee. It boiled a little too long, but neither man complained, and as they sipped the black, thick liquid, they seemed to reach a kind of understanding, like any other Greek men sitting together over coffee. Mark smiled to himself. It was almost archaic, he thought as he relaxed and decided to flow with the masculine tide. "Have you always lived on Kavos?" he asked.

"I was born here seventy years ago. It was much different then."

Listening from the kitchen, Alexa suppressed a smile. She doubted if Kavos had changed in centuries, much less in seventy short years.

As the two men conversed, she didn't stop to wonder at Mark's perfect Greek—she'd expected it. He was a scholar, not a plumber, after all.

"Then you were here during the war?" Mark was asking.

The old man grunted an affirmative response, clearly not willing to engage further in this line of questioning.

"During the German occupation?" Mark persisted.

"Those were terrible times," was the answer.

"But the Greeks were always brave," Mark reminded him.

"That is true," Vassili responded.

"I know there was considerable resistance in this part of the Aegean."

The old man nodded.

"And collaboration, too," Mark ventured.

Alexa almost got into the conversation then, wanting to reprimand Mark, but not sure how to proceed. It was too late in any case. Vassili had drained his cup and stood up.

"Thank you for the coffee, Alexa. Enjoy the fish," he said, picking up his hat and heading for the door.

Alexa followed him and returned moments later with a definite scowl on her face.

"I guess I chased him away. I'm sorry," Mark said not very sincerely.

Alexa silently rinsed the cups before remarking, "Vassili is a little difficult sometimes, but you have to remember that the islanders are very proud people. I'm sure they won't want to hear of collaboration with the Nazis."

"It happened, Alexa."

"Perhaps," she said, "but I don't really want to hear about it, either."

"Didn't your grandfather discuss the war with you?"

"Not much," she responded. "I was only a child. It was all so long ago, Mark."

"Yet for some people, it seems like yesterday," he commented.

For a moment Alexa was silent, a little puzzled. Then she glanced at her watch and said quickly, "We should get back to work. I'll be in the garden if you need anything."

Before he could respond she was gone.

Alexa spent all afternoon trying to clear one section of the garden. It was difficult because she couldn't differentiate between the flowers and the weeds. Finally she made her own rule: if there was a blossom, it qualified as a flower and remained, otherwise, out it went.

As she was digging with her trowel, Alexa felt the edge of something hard. Carefully she loosened the soil, feeling with her fingers as she worked. After almost half an hour of exploration, she realized that she'd come upon a little fountain. It had a large bowl in the middle surrounded by carved figures that she finally decided were birds.

Excitedly Alexa brushed the dirt away until the little fountain emerged. She imagined that this must be the way excavators felt at discovering some long-lost work of art. Her find was only a fountain, but it pleased her just the same. She vowed to clean it up and make it the centerpiece of the garden.

Not now, though. It was late afternoon, the hottest part of the day, and she'd been crouched in the same position for what seemed like hours. Her back ached. Her legs ached. It was time for a swim.

Alexa gathered up her gardening tools, put them in the shed and went inside to change into her suit. She couldn't wait to feel the first cold rush of the sea against her hot skin.

Mark was amazed that he'd gotten along so well. He'd managed to hook up the fixtures by carefully remembering the order in which he'd undone them. The bathroom still had a long way to go, however—new floor, grouting around the tub, tiled shower stall, a coat of paint on the walls. Several coats, he decided as he looked around.

The ache between his shoulder blades that had earlier been barely noticeable was really beginning to bother him. And there was a blister forming on his thumb. He was definitely not in shape for this kind of manual labor, yet he enjoyed it. He could see the actual physical proof of his day's work, and he was damned proud.

While he'd done a good job on the bathroom, he hadn't gotten very far with Alexa. She'd clammed up when he'd asked about the war. Well, he'd ask again, and next time he'd be more subtle.

Alexa paused in the doorway, watching Mark as he surveyed his work. She smiled. He certainly seemed pleased with himself, and enjoying the work was half the battle. The other half, of course, was capability, and from what she could tell, so far he passed that test, too.

"So what do you think?"

Evidently Mark had seen her out of the corner of his eye, but he still hadn't turned around completely. As she walked into the room, his gaze remained on his handiwork and not on her. Another good sign, Alexa thought.

She inspected what he had done carefully, turning on the faucet and flushing the toilet. "Looks good," she said not without surprise. "Everything's in working order."

"Is that disbelief I see?" he asked, noting the look on her face.

"Possibly," she admitted. "I really wasn't sure you'd be able to pull it off."

"Well, one swallow doesn't make a summer, but I've managed so far. Now, about the tile—"

"I'll consider it," she said.

"In the long run, it'll be worth the investment, and tile isn't that expensive here in the islands."

"I know," Alexa said, her mind beginning to wander. It had been a long day, and she was looking forward to a plunge in the cold sea. Very little else was on her mind—unless she counted Mark, who was invading her senses more than she cared to admit.

"Would you like to go for a swim?" she found herself asking.

"It's not even five o'clock," he said. "A true islander would just be getting up from his afternoon nap and ready to work six more hours."

"We're neither of us true islanders," Alexa reminded him.

Mark nodded. He was looking intently at her, and Alexa wasn't sure whether he was noticing the outline of her bathing suit under the oversized shirt she was wearing or whether his eyes were looking through her, reading her thoughts. Well, if the latter was the case, he must really be confused, Alexa decided. She couldn't even define her thoughts herself.

"Oh, you don't have a suit," she reminded him, relieved.

"Don't worry. I can go without," Mark teased, but before she could blush he added, "or wear my shorts. They'll dry out quickly." He smiled into her eyes. "Which would you prefer?"

Without answering, Alexa tossed him the extra towel she'd brought along and headed for the door.

Mark was right behind her.

Chapter 3

Alexa moved quickly along the steep path that led through the olive groves to the little cove nestled among the rocks almost a hundred feet below. Mark managed to keep up with her, although she was goat-like in her agility, maneuvering in and out of the trees and up and down the rocky trail.

He tried to make conversation as they walked, but it wasn't easy. She would rush ahead, wait for him and then rush ahead again. Finally he managed to catch up as she made a turn around a particularly precipitous outcropping of rock.

"Are the olive trees still bearing?" he asked when they paused just past the grove.

"I think so, but I haven't gotten the hang of picking them yet."

That was Mark's opportunity to start a conversation. "There's a knack to it," he confided. "You take a long stick and beat on the branches until the olives fall off.''

"And then go rummaging around on the ground to pick them up?" she asked a little skeptically.

"No," he contradicted her. "The Greeks do it easily by spreading sheets on the ground to catch the olives."

Alexa paused a moment to think about that. It seemed both primitive and effective. "Are you sure?" she asked.

"Absolutely. I'm an authority on the subject. Did you know that olive trees live over a thousand years?" At the moment Mark wasn't remotely interested in olives, but he was very interested in Alexa, the way her eyes sparkled as she turned to look back at him, the way her body seemed to come alive with interest, too. She was a remarkable-looking woman. The more time he spent with her the more attractive he found her.

"That can't be true," she said.

"I guarantee it," Mark answered, watching her reaction.

She'd waited a split second too long before turning back toward the trail, and in that time she momentarily lost her footing. Mark was there beside her, reaching for her arm, steadying her.

"It's true," he said, almost forgetting the subject as he held on to her arm longer, much longer, than necessary, his face only inches from hers. There were faint beads of perspiration on her forehead. Her hair was damp around her face, and her cheeks were flushed. But he really only noticed her lips. They were parted slightly as her breath came in short, sweet spurts.

"You'll have to learn to trust me," he said, but he wasn't talking about the facts of harvesting olives.

Alexa didn't respond but turned, tossed her head and continued on her way, this time walking more carefully, avoiding the tangles in the undergrowth that had caught her foot earlier.

"It's tough going now," she said, needlessly, Mark thought, for the incline was obvious. "There are some footholds, though."

"I'll go first," he offered.

"Nope. I'm used to it." She clambered down rapidly as if to make up for her earlier clumsiness, and Mark stood above, watching. She was surefooted and quick, and once more he marveled at her agility, but not before marveling at her looks, which had kept him intrigued much of the day. There was something about her that was difficult to analyze. She wasn't as stunning as other women he'd known, neither pretty as a model nor studiedly striking. Yet he still couldn't stop looking at her.

"Race you to the surf," she called out, and before he could take his eyes away from her and respond, she was off, shedding her shoes and floppy shirt as she ran.

By the time Mark had scrambled down to the beach, Alexa was at the water's edge. As he watched, she dove beneath a wave and then emerged, sleek and cool and very tempting.

Pulling off his shirt and shoes, Mark followed her into the water. It hit him like a jolt of electricity.

"Invigorating, isn't it?" Alexa called out.

"Freezing," was Mark's response as he attempted to swim a few strokes toward her.

"You'll get used to it," she told him, "if you go in every day."

"Assuming I survive this," Mark replied, "I'll consider going in every day." He drew up next to Alexa and turned to float on his back, looking at the blue sky. "There's nothing in the world quite the color of the sky over Greece, is there?"

"And there's no air as clear or sun as bright—or people as independent," she added.

"You're not without an independent streak yourself," he remarked. "I assume it comes from the Greek side of your family."

"Definitely," she agreed as they swam side by side, easily, with even strokes, toward a spit of land that jutted out from the cove. "I'll race you," she called out, showing a little of her independent nature. And showing a little foresight as well, for by the time she'd made the challenge, she was halfway to her destination, and Mark had his work cut out catching up with her.

Ahead of them swam several dolphins, and as he cut through the water beside Alexa, Mark realized that he hadn't felt so happy in months or even in years, certainly not in his work. This was a different kind of sensation for him, and he let himself enjoy it.

The dolphins leapt high into the air, playful, showing off for the two strange forms that swam among them. Mark and Alexa laughed at their antics, and the dolphins seemed to be laughing back as they cavorted in the water, making the high-pitched sounds that were, Mark said, part of their own special language.

"They say dolphins are more like humans than any other mammal," Alexa remarked.

"They're certainly the most fun-loving," Mark decided, trying to hide his disappointment as Alexa turned and began to swim back toward shore. He could easily have spent the rest of the day in their aquatic adventure.

His disappointment faded somewhat as they reached the shore and walked for a while along the beach in companionable silence, feeling one with nature and with the special beauty that was Greece. Alexa seemed a part of that beauty, like some glorious young goddess, tanned and long-legged, with a slim figure that was almost boyish except for the delicious curve of her waist and rise of her breasts.

By the time they started back up the hill, Mark had thought of a way to extend their time together.

"What are you going to do with that fish Vassili brought you?" he asked as the path widened enough for them to walk side by side.

"Cook it, I guess," Alexa answered.

"Tonight?"

"I suppose so. Fish doesn't keep very long, and I certainly don't want to end up throwing it away. Vassili gets livid over that kind of waste." She paused for a moment, and Mark quickly stepped in.

"I suppose you have some good recipes for cooking fish."

"Actually I don't. As I mentioned before, my culinary talents stop right after sandwiches."

"We could grill it," Mark suggested, "with a little lemon juice and olive oil. For that kind of fish, nothing tastes quite so good."

"We?"

"Well . . ." He smiled.

"I suppose you know exactly how to do it?"

They'd reached the top of the hill and Mark answered confidently as he followed Alexa through the garden into the house. "It's been said that my grilled fish rivals any in the Mediterranean."

Alexa laughed. "And the Aegean, as well?"

"Goes without saying. Would it be presumptuous if I invited myself for dinner?"

"I think you already have."

"I'll get a fire started."

"All right. I'll change and then make a salad. There's fresh bread."

"And cheese?" he asked.

"Always."

As she left him at the grill and went into her room, Alexa wondered how all this had happened. He'd changed from employee to guest during a swim in the Aegean. That wasn't a good way to begin a working relationship. Yet it seemed ridiculous to tell him that she wanted to have dinner alone when she certainly didn't. After all, it was just two people sharing a meal.

Then why was she spending so much time deciding what to wear? A little annoyed at herself, Alexa pulled a pair of shorts and T-shirt from the drawer and quickly put them on. Then she took extra time to blow-dry her hair, telling herself that she would have done that, anyway.

Mark hadn't been exaggerating—the fish was perfect, light and delicate with just the right touch of oil and lemon. Alexa managed to come up with a halfway decent salad and, as she admitted to Mark, even she couldn't do any harm to the rest of the meal—fresh bread, feta cheese and retsina. To Alexa's surprise and delight, Mark was also a big fan of the wine.

"Not many foreigners like retsina," Alexa said as she poured him a second glass.

"I know," Mark answered. "There're quite a few Greeks who aren't too fond of it, either. Maybe I'm just a romantic." He looked at her and smiled and then reached out and touched his glass to hers.

They were sitting in the garden beneath a low blanket of stars, surrounded by the night sounds of the islands, and just the word "romantic" made Alexa a little nervous in this night that was so totally that way already.

She quickly tried to diffuse the mood. "I don't think retsina is what you'd call a romantic wine. The taste came about by accident, really."

"Oh?"

Alexa wasn't sure whether Mark knew about the wine or not, but now that she'd gotten herself into the subject, she kept going. "A merchant in the early days mistakenly stored his wine in pine barrels. The result was what we have here, resin blended with fermented grape."

"Sounds terrible," Mark said. "But," he added as he took a sip, "it *tastes…*romantic." He looked across at her with a smile. "In spite of your pragmatic explanation. There's another theory, you know." He paused, still looking at her.

Alexa felt uneasy beneath his steady gaze. "I assume you're going to tell me."

"Just building the proper suspense," Mark commented smugly. When he noticed the beginnings of a smile on Alexa's lips, he went on, encouraged. "I prefer the legend of the brave, resourceful and *independent* Greeks," he said with a grin, "who deliberately spoiled their wine by dumping resin in it to upset the palates of the conquering Turks. Just one of many schemes to free themselves of foreign domination."

"An interesting theory, I must admit, but I hope you don't put tourism in the foreign domination category," she joked, "or there goes my livelihood."

"And, temporarily, mine as well. No, I don't think ill of tourists, and I wish you great success in your venture."

"So after your first day you're not totally discouraged?"

"Over all, it went pretty well, I'd say. What's on the agenda for tomorrow, boss?"

Alexa relaxed at the mention of their day's work, a subject she could easily handle. "I'll find out from Aunt Sophie where to get the least expensive tile, and you can keep working on the bathroom and—"

"Aunt Sophie?"

"She's my great aunt, actually, Pappous's sister. She's quite remarkable."

"I'd like to meet her."

Alexa laughed. "You won't be able to avoid it. As soon as she hears you're working for me, she'll be over to check you out."

"I'll be on my best behavior," Mark promised.

There was something a little intimate about that remark, and Alexa tried to change the subject, but it seemed that no matter how they started out, Mark always managed to get personal. At one point she even found herself explaining her name.

"Cord certainly isn't a Greek name," Mark observed, "unless it was changed. Is your father Greek?"

"No, my mother's is the Greek side, but Dad's Greek by adoption, he always says. He went along with Mom on observing holidays like Greek Easter and even in choosing our names."

"Alexa? Sure," Mark said, answering his own question. "It's feminine for Alexi."

"Yes, that was my grandfather's name. I guess you know all the complicated ways of getting Greek names. The first son is named for the father's father and the second son for the mother's father."

"Yes," Mark answered. "Conversely the first daughter is named for the mother's mother, the second for the father's mother. So how did you get to be named for your grandfather?" he asked, a little puzzled.

"Well, my two sisters captured the first names, and then when I came along, the doctors told Mom there'd be no more children. Which meant no sons. So I was named Alexa Danielle. Alexa for my grandfather Coumanis and Danielle for my grandfather Daniel Cord. But Pappous always ignored the Danielle and insisted I was named for him. I guess I became the favorite."

Mark could certainly understand that.

"I believe that's why he left me the house."

"And thus your adventures in Greece began."

"Continued, really," she corrected him. "They actually began long ago when I first came to this island as a child."

"And so they continue," he agreed softly. "And now I'm part of them."

He was doing it again, moving into her personal life, making it seem as though they shared something. He was insidious, this Mark Everett. She'd have to watch him, be sure he kept strictly to business.

That was difficult tonight with the moon so bright above them. It was up to her to be professional, so Alexa stood up and said briskly, "We have a long, hard day ahead, and I need to turn in."

Seemingly unperturbed, Mark stood up, too. "Thanks for supplying the dinner."

"Thanks for cooking it."

"It was my pleasure," he said sincerely. "See you tomorrow."

"Early," she reminded him.

"I'll be here, Alexa. As I've said before, you have to learn to trust me."

Not only did she trust him, she also took his advice, not a usual occurrence for Alexa. The next day she found herself walking along the cobbled streets of Kavos, the tiles in her string bag clinking with each step. Mark had suggested decorative tiles for the bathroom, and Sophie had told her where to purchase them at the best price. She'd taken a bus at the harbor and traveled into the hills in search of the family workshop that Sophie had suggested.

Finding the Contakos family hadn't been an easy task, but there was no doubt it had been worth the trip. The tiles were beautiful, more attractive than the renowned ones on the island of Rhodes. Mark's idea had been right on target, so much so that she was beginning to wonder how she could finagle her budget to buy more and use them in the kitchen, too.

As Alexa walked, she couldn't resist fantasizing about having a special tile made with her initials, A.C., the same as her grandfather's, entwined with the image of an island flower. Getting into her fantasy, she was trying to decide just which flower to choose as she reached the house, pushed open the gate and saw Mark sitting on the steps that led to the kitchen.

At the rate he was working, Alexa wouldn't be able to afford any tile at all, much less her own personal symbol.

She glanced pointedly at her watch. It was only three o'clock. "Taking a break?" she asked, trying to remain casual.

"An unanticipated one," Mark responded hesitantly. It was clear that he didn't want to explain.

"Should I be alarmed?" she asked, already aware from the look on his face and the tone in his voice, that alarm was justified.

"I'm afraid so," he admitted.

Alexa waited, and when Mark's silence became unbearable, she sank down beside him. "Tell me."

"I don't want to be an alarmist, but I'm afraid there's some dry rot in the wood framing."

"All of it?" she asked numbly. The house was made of stone, but she knew that the frames and the rafters beneath the tiled roof were wood.

"I'm not sure," he answered. "I discovered it when I was painting the bathroom ceiling. It looks like water dripped through the roof and rotted the beams above the bath."

"And maybe above all the other rooms."

"It's possible," he admitted. "The roof—and the rafters—may have to be replaced."

Alexa knew that the tile roof would be expensive, but nothing like the cost of new rafters. There wasn't much timber left on Kavos, or any of the Greek islands, for that matter. They had all been stripped bare long ago, the once-wooded areas left to the mountain goats.

This is what she'd feared, an unanticipated catastrophe coming out of nowhere and ruining all of her plans. Alexa felt as if she'd been hit in the stomach. "What can we do?" she asked.

"I can go back up and examine the rafters. Maybe..."

His voice drifted off, and Alexa knew it was hopeless. Unbidden tears came to her eyes. She tried quickly to wipe them away, but Mark saw the drops and put his arm around her.

The warmth of his caring touch somehow helped, but his empathy wouldn't be enough to keep her bank account from vanishing with this problem. "I might as well admit defeat and give up, go back home," she said, adding bitterly, "I can just write this off as another failure."

"It wouldn't be a complete loss," he said. "You could sell the house."

"Nobody's going to buy this wreck."

"Maybe they will," he said. "The acreage is beautiful, and so is the view. It could be a good investment, a perfect fixer-upper for a wealthy European or American. You could advertise," he went on, but Alexa wasn't listening.

She hardly noticed when he left, but moments later he returned, bringing with him a bottle of wine. He opened it and poured her a glass. "I feel terrible for you," he said in a voice that was gentle and comforting. "I would do anything to help."

"Would you lend me a few thousand?" she asked with a wry smile before she started to sob.

Looking down at her, Mark saw that Alexa's eyes were filled with pain, and he reached out to touch her damp cheeks where the tears had begun to overflow her eyes. "Maybe it was just an impossible dream, Alexa," he said softly.

"Maybe," she agreed. Then, moments later, she shook her head, and Mark saw that the tears had stopped. There was something else in her eyes—fire, determination. "No," she said firmly, "I can't stand giving up. I won't do it, not again."

"You're really determined, aren't you?"

"Yes, I am," she answered, not quite sure where the determination would lead but strengthened by it.

"I have a suggestion," he told her, "something that could work."

"Tell me," she said. "I'm game for anything at this point."

"I could move in."

"*Oriste?*" she asked, speaking Greek suddenly, as if she hadn't understood the offer he'd made in English.

"I mean just what I said. Let me move in with you, Alexa."

"That's a very interesting suggestion, Mark, but it hardly solves my problem."

He managed to laugh. "I'm not being lascivious, just logical. Think about it for a minute, Alexa. You're paying me a moderate salary. In turn, I'm paying rent to Niko for the room in his taverna." She started to interrupt, but Mark held up his hand. "Let me finish. Now think what would happen if you subtracted the rent I pay Niko from my salary and let me live here. It would save me a long walk," he said with a smile, "and it would save you a great deal of money, maybe enough over time to afford lumber for the roof."

He paused to let her respond, which she did, finally. "I suppose that could work. If we add the money I'd save to what I have on hand. Right now, I can't even remember how much that is. All I know is that it's fast disappearing."

"Then give my plan a try, Alexa."

"Why would you want to do it?" she asked, trying to keep the suspicion out of her voice.

"I told you, to save the walk." He smiled ingratiatingly. "And, to tell the truth, that taverna can be very noisy. This way, I save whatever I make and put it against a boat ticket to my next stop along the way. The view is also much better than that alley behind Niko's place."

This time she had to smile. What he said made sense, but Alexa still wasn't sure how to handle it, or how much it would help if she could handle it. "I need some time to think," she told him.

"Sure," he said. "I can understand that. Do you want me to leave you alone now?" He touched her shoulder in a gesture that was both understanding and somehow comforting.

"Yes," she answered softly.

"I'm sorry about all this, Alexa."

"I know. Thanks." She smiled, and he squeezed her shoulder before turning to pick up his knapsack and go out the door, leaving Alexa alone with a sudden, terrible sadness.

She got up and moved to the window, looking out over the olive trees, tears forming in her eyes again. This was her grandfather's house, his land. How could she give it up? Moving away from the window, Alexa walked slowly through the rooms of the house, touching familiar things that had belonged to him. Lingering in the living room, she opened the desk drawer and reached for a letter, the one that had been attached to her grandfather's will.

She sank into an overstuffed chair in the corner where he always used to sit, reading by the last light of the afternoon, and opened the letter again.

Dear Alexa,

When you read this I will be gone, but I can rest easy knowing that you will be living in my house. I brought your grandmother here as a bride. My children were born here. The house endured through the years, even during the Nazi occupation when terrible deeds were done.

You will give the house a new life, and you will learn all of its secrets. Remember your heritage, remember the past and the legends of Greece. Take care not only of the house but also of my garden. I loved it well, and in it you will find the secret of life.

Remember you are my beloved grandchild, and
I entrust our heritage to you.

The tears brimmed again and spilled down her
cheeks. "I won't fail you, Pappous," she whispered.
"Somehow I'll find a way."

Alexa left the house then, and not even closing the
door behind her, went out through the gate and down
the hill. She didn't stop until she reached her aunt's
house.

"Child, what is it?" Sophie asked. "You look as if
you've run all the way. Has something happened?"

Alexa nodded and sat down at the kitchen table
where Sophie had been having her coffee. There, her
tears spent, she explained what Mark had discovered.

"You must not leave the island," Sophie said simply when she'd heard everything. "You *cannot* leave
because you belong here." Sophie leaned back, fold-
ing her ample arms across her equally ample bosom.
"Your mother went to America for safety when the
war broke out, and when she returned, we knew that
we'd lost her. But when she brought you back, Alexa,
I knew that someday you would be here for good."

"I guess I always knew that, too, although I never
realized it until Pappous left me the house. Even then,
I was really afraid to say how much I loved it for fear
I might lose it." She smiled sadly. "Now it looks like
the time has come."

"No," Sophie said adamantly. "We won't let that
happen. We'll find a solution."

"There is one possibility," Alexa admitted. "Mark,
the worker I just hired, suggested that he move into the
house and deduct the rent from his salary. That would

certainly help, but I don't know what people will think.''

"Do you care, Alexa?"

Alexa shrugged. She didn't really.

"Then do not worry. Because you are still considered an American, you will not be judged so harshly by the gossiping old women," Sophie said reassuringly, "but even if that were not so, it's what you feel that matters, not what others think."

Alexa agreed, relieved at Sophie's assessment. "But even saving on Mark's salary, I'm just not sure that would be enough."

"Maybe I can help with the timber that you will need," Sophie said.

"Aunt Sophie, I can't take money from you."

Sophie laughed throatily. "No, my child, you cannot, as I have very little to offer. Like my brother, all my wealth is in my home and in my friends. Among those friends, however, there happens to be one who has been in my debt for almost twenty years. I will never collect. This he knows, and this I know. However," Sophie said emphatically, leaning across the table toward Alexa, "his brother-in-law owns a lumberyard on Samos. So perhaps there is a way to collect on the debt by seeing to it that you get your timber for a good price."

"Oh, Sophie," Alexa said, "you're not going to give up on me, are you?"

"Nor will I let you give up on yourself. Find out how much timber you need and let me know. Then tell that young man you will accept his offer."

Alexa got up and moved around the table to give Sophie a hug. "I will," she said with relief.

"And Alexa," Sophie called out as the younger woman headed toward the door, "tell the Englishman that I will be up to meet him soon. On Kavos we know how to take care of our own, so you might also remind him that many eyes will be watching."

Alexa made her way down the hill toward the harbor just as the sun touched the horizon. The fishermen had brought in the day's catch and sat huddled together at tables outside the taverna drinking their ouzo and retsina. Niko stood in the doorway, and when he saw Alexa he called out.

"*Kalispera*, Alexa. Good evening and welcome. Come in and have a glass of wine and tell us how the young man I sent to you is getting along. He is a good worker, is he not?" Niko was in the habit of answering his own questions with yet another question.

"Yes, he is, and I thank you, Niko, but I must talk to Mark now. Is he in his room?"

"I believe so," Niko said. "I will call him for you." Niko was curious about what Alexa might have to say to the Englishman. Besides, Alexa knew that he didn't approve of her going up to the room alone and causing talk among his cronies. At the moment she didn't care in the slightest. She had other things besides propriety on her mind.

"No, thanks, Niko. I'll go up and get him." Alexa headed around the building, dodging the trash cans, and climbed the narrow stairs in back to the second landing. She hesitated a moment and then knocked on the door.

"Just a minute," Mark called out, and Alexa imagined that he was surprised to have a visitor, and more surprised, she noticed when he opened the door, that she was the visitor.

After a split second's pause, he asked, ''Won't you come in?''

That presented a problem. Alexa certainly didn't want to talk to him standing out on the tiny landing. On the other hand, she didn't feel entirely comfortable going into his room. Besides, one of the waiters was down below in the alley on his break, smoking a cigarette and watching.

''Please,'' Mark said, holding the door open and giving her very little choice. During her moment of hesitation, Alexa had glanced at him and saw that he looked very different from the Mark who worked at her house. His hair was tousled, as if he'd been running his hands through it, and he was wearing reading glasses.

''I've just been working on some translations,'' he explained, taking off his glasses and offering Alexa a chair.

From downstairs she could hear the noise of the kitchen staff, clattering pots and pans and talking over their own din. It was definitely not an ideal setting in which to work.

Her own silence finally prompted Mark to ask, ''Is this the place in the script where you fire me?''

Alexa returned his smile and retorted, ''No, it's the place where I come to ask you to move in with me. I might add I've never made that offer to a man before.'' Knowing that Mark turned every remark she made into something personal, Alexa couldn't for the life of her imagine why she'd said such a thing. She blushed in spite of her usual disinclination to be embarrassed by anything, and at his wicked smile she blushed even more.

Fortunately Mark did nothing more than smile before asking seriously, "You decided that my idea was a good one?"

"I decided it was the only one," she said, "particularly since I have no intention of giving up."

"Good girl," he said encouragingly. "What made you change your mind?"

"My family," she said. "I talked to Aunt Sophie, and then I reread a letter from my grandfather that was attached to his will. It made me realize how valuable the house is. There's a wonderful secret in there, Mark."

His look confused her at first until she realized that he didn't really understand. "Oh, I'm sure the secret Pappous referred to is the secret of happiness. Maybe it can be found in something specific that's there within the walls or maybe it exists by just being there. Whatever he meant, I'm sure I'll know someday. At any rate, I mean to stay and find out. I'm not going to leave."

"Then I'll help you, Alexa. Tonight I'll let Niko know I'm leaving, and I'll move in tomorrow morning.

Chapter 4

Alexa was thinking about rolling out of bed when she heard Mark's voice.

"Hey, come on. Rise and shine. It's breakfast time."

She was tired. It had been a difficult but very rewarding two weeks, and the tiredness was almost welcome for it brought with it a kind of exhilaration, a feeling that they were getting somewhere.

But that didn't make getting up at six in the morning any easier.

"I'm on my way," Alexa called out as she swung her feet over the side of the bed, actually smiling to herself in spite of the early hour.

As she went into the bathroom, splashed cold water on her face, brushed her teeth and tried to wake up, Alexa thought about the routine she and Mark had fallen into. Gone was the employer-employee relationship. Instead they were working as two friends involved in a project that meant everything to her and seemed to mean almost as much to him. He was her ally. It was so much easier than she'd expected, so much more fun. For the first time in a long while, she had hopes that her dream to turn Pappous's house into a hotel would actually happen, and even more unbelievable, she would enjoy every moment along the way.

Alexa ran a brush through her hair as Mark called out once more. Every day, when breakfast was ready, he got very urgent about it. "Has to be eaten when it's still warm or all my culinary efforts go to waste," he'd told her again and again. They'd reached an easy compromise with meals: he made breakfast, she handled lunch, usually sandwiches or soup, and they shared dinner with Mark solving the real cooking problems and Alexa satisfied to take care of the menial chores.

"I'm on the way," she called out as she pulled on her shorts and a canary-yellow T-shirt and headed for the kitchen.

The sun had a way of brightening everything in the Greek mornings, especially the airy kitchen of her big house. Alexa stopped for a moment in the doorway and watched as Mark, serious in the completion of his breakfast duties, concentrated on whatever he was fixing on the stove.

Sophie had been right when she'd come by to pass judgment on Mark. After letting Alexa know that she approved of the nice young man, she'd added that if she'd known he was so good-looking he might have been working for her instead of Alexa, and Alexa had to agree with her appraisal.

Mark's hair was bleached a pale blond by the sun, and his dark tan made his eyes seem bluer than ever. He'd adapted well to his job and the island. He looked as if he belonged in Greece. When he turned and smiled at her, Alexa couldn't help but feel a catch in her breath, a skip in her heartbeat. Yes, Sophie was right, even though Alexa had no intention of admitting that to her aunt.

Alexa sat down at the table and drank the juice Mark had put before her as he worked, whistling happily at the stove. She couldn't keep from thinking how intimate this morning scene had become, how warm and easy, as if they were a couple who'd been together for years.

Except of course that there was no intimacy, and they had only known each other a short time, so the warmth was probably only in her imagination. Certainly Mark hadn't ever crossed over the line between employer and employee, even though his ability to get her to talk about herself in a more personal way than she'd ever done before continued. Otherwise they shared the house and the work, and that was that.

At times, Alexa had allowed herself to fantasize a little about what it might be like if they crossed that invisible line, but she always remembered that they were both here for a reason: she to transform the house into a working inn, he to earn enough wages to move on to the next island or the next continent in his nomadic search.

"*Voilà,* French toast," Mark said, setting Alexa's plate before her and interrupting her reverie.

Alexa took a bite and exclaimed, "It's marvelous. Maybe we should appoint you chef for every meal."

"No way," Mark said. "Breakfast and a few suggestions for the grill about exhausts my culinary expertise. Now eat up."

Alexa took another bite and tried to stifle a yawn.

"Sleepy?" he asked. "That is, sleepier than usual?"

Alexa laughed. "I know, mornings aren't my best times, but I do feel particularly tired today. For some reason I kept waking during the night. Thought I heard you rambling around."

"Sorry," he said. "I'm not a very good sleeper, and I often wake up and read."

"I could have sworn I heard you downstairs."

"Raiding the pantry? Guilty," he admitted with a smile.

"Ordinarily I probably wouldn't have heard anything since I sleep like a log, but last night—"

"Worries about the house are probably getting to you," he said.

"I guess, even though everything seems fine at the moment. Aunt Sophie said the lumber is on the way. It was loaded on the ferry from Samos yesterday, so that's one hurdle crossed, but I keep thinking there's something else I don't know about yet, something that can't be anticipated, some catastrophe just waiting to happen."

"That's not the way to think, Alexa," he advised. "It's true that you need to be realistic, examine all the possibilities, but you can't be defeatist. Besides, it may actually work out better for you in the long run not to go on with this venture. Only time will tell."

"Is that some sort of Aristotelian reasoning?"

Mark laughed. "In a way, I suppose. At any rate, we don't have time to wait around for a catastrophe.

There's plenty of work to do until the timber arrives, so we'd better get on with it.''

He gave her a little push and then tousled her hair in a way that was friendly, almost chummy, and definitely personal. It made her feel suddenly happy and very young.

Alexa couldn't believe that her luck had been so good. Mark hadn't needed to replace all the rafters, so they had timber left over for other emergencies, which, in spite of his scolding, Alexa couldn't keep from anticipating. Even more surprising, she had found herself helping Mark retile the roof, which meant conquering her objection to ladders.

"I just try not to look down," she told him as she scurried to the rooftop.

"Well, I won't put you through it again if you'll just hand me the last few tiles."

"Gladly," Alexa said, inching her way toward him.

Mark held out his hand. "Come on over here, Alexa. I won't let you fall."

Gingerly she did as she was told, and less than an hour later, the job was finished. Sitting beside Mark, straddling the roof, Alexa exclaimed, "You can't even tell where we patched."

"We?"

Alexa laughed. "I'll admit my talents are more evident on the ground. So now if you'll help me down, I'm going into the hills and dig up some wildflowers."

"What for?" Mark asked as he took her hand and led her across the roof.

"To replenish my garden. I finally finished the weeding, and now I'm left with bare spots to fill in."

Mark helped Alexa onto the ladder and watched as she carefully climbed down, breathing a sigh of relief when her feet hit solid ground.

"Do you think they'll live?" Mark asked as he joined her.

"I have no idea," Alexa admitted, "but it's worth a try."

Mark was unaccustomedly quiet as Alexa gathered her gardening tools, and then he surprised her by asking to go along. "I probably won't be any help since I don't know the difference between a poppy and a peony, but if you'd like some company..."

It wasn't as if they never saw each other—they were together all day, every day. Mark couldn't believe that he'd asked to go with Alexa to dig up flowers, a chore that didn't interest him in the least. He realized that he was becoming more and more attracted to her and had to admit it was difficult to let her out of his sight.

Alexa nodded, a little perplexed, he thought, but then he was also perplexed and could offer nothing in the way of an explanation as they headed up into the hills, the wildflowers forming a carpet of yellow, blue, red, lavender and pale pink beneath their feet.

"Do you know what any of these are?" he asked.

"The truth?"

"Yes."

"I haven't the faintest idea, but they'll look beautiful in the garden," Alexa said as they began to dig up flowers at random, leaving large clumps of root and soil for transplanting. "I don't think it's necessary to know their names in order to get them to grow. It just takes a green thumb.''

''Which I hope you have,'' he said, placing a big batch of bright red flowers in the basket.

''We'll know soon enough,'' Alexa said with a laugh.

They spent part of the afternoon among the wildflowers, and when she became exhausted, Alexa finally dropped down in a field of yellow flowers, stretching out on her back, arms above her head. Mark sat down beside her and looked over, noticing that her eyes were closed and her dark lashes were sooty against cheeks that were pinkened by the sun. He continued to watch her, happy for a chance to stare outright and not be worried about her reaction.

In the sunlight her dark hair was streaked with auburn and gold, yet her brows and lashes were almost black, as dark as her Greek eyes, eyes that she must have inherited from her mother.

Mark let his gaze wander down the length of her body, lingering on the fullness of her breasts outlined by the T-shirt, her flat stomach, marvelously curved hips and her long, slim legs. There was a scratch on one of them that she'd gotten scrambling through bushes, and it made her seem vulnerable.

I thought you'd be pretty, Alexa Cord. I expected that, he said to himself, not daring to speak aloud for fear she wasn't quite asleep. *I just didn't know that I would like you so damn much. That makes it very tough, dear Alexa.*

But tough or not, he could hardly resist the temptation of her full, sensuous lips. For a moment he felt himself leaning toward her as if to kiss them. He stopped just in time, as she opened her eyes.

"I thought you were sleeping," he said softly.

"No, it's much too uncomfortable," Alexa answered, sitting up and brushing at her clothes. "Fields of flowers always look so luscious and inviting from a distance, like soft beds. But they're not," she exclaimed.

"Yet you look beautiful among them," Mark couldn't help observing. "The flowers—whatever they're called—are just about the color of your T-shirt."

Alexa smiled, and Mark felt his breath catch in his throat. He reached out and touched her hand, and when she smiled again he wondered if he would be able to resist taking her into his arms.

"Unfortunately," Alexa said, "they're very prickly."

"I can solve that," Mark said, trying to keep his emotions out of his voice, although it was difficult. He knew there was a huskiness that gave him away.

"How?" she asked.

"Well, not by any sort of magic, just by a strategic move. See that clump of grass over by the trees? It looks very comfortable from here, and I'll bet you it's not as deceiving as the flowers."

"You're on," she said, and then changed her mind. "But we'd better be getting back with these flowers before they wilt."

"They can wait a little while longer. Come on," he insisted. "We have a bet." His hand was still touching hers, and he held on tightly and pulled her to her feet.

Alexa followed him to the trees.

"All right. Give it a try," he told her.

Carefully she sat down and then stretched out on her back. It was comfortable—soft and fresh and sweet-smelling. "Not bad," she admitted.

"Not bad?" Mark exclaimed as he lay down beside her. "It's a wonderful spot—and a wonderful day. Some of the best times of my life have been spent here in Greece," he said thoughtfully, remembering moments of innocence and beauty that were so far away and long ago that he'd never expected to recapture them. Yet today that seemed almost possible.

"You came here as a student?"

"Even before," he told her. "When I was a kid, my godfather brought me to Greece almost every summer, usually to the Peloponnisos or Crete but sometimes to the islands. He was an archeologist and he let me putter around with him. Obviously a very patient man," Mark added.

Alexa was watching him thoughtfully and listening in a way that he didn't remember a woman ever doing before. In his experience, they often seemed preoccupied with themselves. But not Alexa. "You inherited your interest in Greek history from him," she said. It wasn't a question but an observation.

"Yes. Mycenaean ruins were his specialty. I grew up on tales of Agamemnon and Odysseus and the Trojan war."

"Pretty hard stuff for a kid."

"You're right. I've never recovered."

Alexa looked over at him, thinking how nice it was to lie down under the shade of the trees, talking so easily, feeling so close. She'd never known this kind of companionship with a man before. It was new and exciting to her, and at the same time, comforting.

"I know a little more about you now," she said, piecing everything together. "Your parents don't really approve of your classical studies, you're a middling good carpenter and a better-than-average plumber."

"Is that it?" he asked, feigning disappointment.

"Let's see. When absolutely necessary, you can tear down rafters and replace a tile roof."

"No more?"

"Oh, yes. Much more. You had an early childhood education in the classics, and you're a very good cook."

"That about covers it," he said with a smile.

"Oh, I don't think so," Alexa answered. There was so much that she didn't know, years and years that hadn't been touched upon. Out of it all, there was one thing, very personal, that she felt compelled to find out.

"Ask away," he offered. "My life's an open book."

She began with a question easily answered. "Do you have any brothers and sisters?"

"Nope. I'm a spoiled only child."

Alexa sat up in the grass beside him, but Mark continued to lie on his back. Not being able to see his face made it easier to form the next question, the one that she'd wanted to ask not just today but for a long time.

"Do you, um, have you ever been...married?" There. Nothing so difficult about that, she thought and turned back to look at him.

He'd moved around, leaning on one elbow, and his eyes met hers directly. For a moment he just looked, deep into her eyes.

"No," he said finally. "Have you?"

"No."

It was quiet then. There was no sound but the droning of a bee. She wanted to go on with this, ask why he'd never married, ask how close he'd come, ask what had prevented it. And then ask what kind of woman he was attracted to. Yet those were schoolgirl questions, especially since they masked what she really wanted to know—how he felt about *her*.

But she didn't ask, couldn't ask. It seemed too personal, and although he frequently managed to get personal with her, Alexa didn't have his nerve.

So she said nothing. Mark, on the other hand, had no compunction about continuing the conversation but in an easy manner that she never would have been able to manage.

"What about all the hearts you've broken along the way?"

"What about them?" she responded flippantly.

"Tell me their sad stories."

Alexa laughed. "Most were so distraught that they threw themselves off cliffs and out of windows."

"I can understand that," he said, and the look he gave her then made Alexa realize that he was doing it again—getting personal with her, inviting those blushes that only seemed to rise to her cheeks when Mark was around.

She got up quickly, reminding him that there was planting to do, and with another grin, he followed her along the path.

"Oh, look at that bush," Alexa said as they crossed a section of crumbling rock fence. "I recognize it even if I don't know the name. It's just like the one next to the wall in my garden.''

''I know the name,'' Mark said proudly. ''It's myrtle.''

''How do you know?'' Alexa asked, passing by the bush, which was much too large to transplant.

''Because it's said to be beloved of the gods and goddesses,'' he told her.

''A scholarly shrub,'' Alexa said with a laugh.

''Of course. That's the only kind I can identify, but I can plant them all, and we'd better get to it if we intend to finish by sundown.''

They didn't quite make it, but the sun had just disappeared, leaving a trail of magenta across the sea, when Alexa announced that the last peony—if that's what it was—was in the ground and thoroughly watered.

''A cause for celebration,'' Mark said, standing up, holding his aching back with one hand. ''How about dinner at Nikos's with wine and dancing?''

''Unfortunately an evening like that isn't in our budget.''

''Forget the budget,'' he advised. ''Dinner's on me.''

''Oh, no, I couldn't,'' Alexa demurred.

''Of course you could. I've saved every penny of my salary since I moved in. Besides, how much can dinner at the taverna cost? It isn't the Ritz, you know.''

''I know, but it seems so extravagant.''

He could tell she was weakening, and once he began talking about it, Mark found he really wanted the evening to happen. He wanted to take her out and be with her in a setting away from work—dance with her, hold her. "Listen, Alexa, we deserve a night on the town. We're becoming as stuffy as old married people, cooking dinner and turning in at nine."

As soon as he said it and saw her look away, Mark realized that he shouldn't have gotten quite so personal as to mention marriage, but it was too late now to take it back. "Come on." He reached out and touched her hand. "Let's celebrate."

"Well, it would be fun."

That was enough for Mark. "I'll shower first and get out of your way." He headed for the house, not giving her a chance to back out.

It wasn't exactly the Ritz, he'd been right about that, but Mark couldn't remember when he'd looked across a table at a woman more beautiful, not even at the Ritz, and he'd been there many times with many beautiful women.

During their time together he'd only seen Alexa in shorts or jeans with T-shirts and occasionally a terry-cloth robe buttoned to the neck. No matter what she wore, she always looked beautiful, but he hadn't been prepared for Alexa dressed up, or for her bright colors of yellow, blue and green. They were her colors, he thought, perfect with her dark eyes and hair, and yet any color would look good on Alexa.

She was asking him something, but he didn't quite hear her because he was too caught up with seeing her. The cotton sundress was cut low in front, and for the first time Mark was able to get a glimpse of her breasts just where her tan line ended. He'd often imagined the soft, creamy skin. It was more inviting than in his fantasies.

"Mark?"

He looked up and realized she was waiting for a response. "Yes," he said, choosing the affirmative answer, a selection which proved to be the wrong one.

"You really prefer to order from the menu?"

"Oh, did I say yes? I meant no." Mark laughed. "Too much sun today, I guess."

"I guess so," Alexa agreed.

"Come on," he said, getting up and taking her hand. "Menus are for tourists. Let's go back to the kitchen and peer in a few pots and see what Niko has to offer."

It was customary at the taverna for Niko's friends to have a look at the specials of the evening, many of which weren't mentioned on the menu but were prepared to order from an abundance of fresh fish and vegetables and pastries. With Niko hovering over them to be sure they didn't miss any of his delicacies, Mark and Alexa made their choices and returned to the table just as the waiter was serving hot bread and a salad of yoghurt and cucumbers called *zazeeki*, which was one of Alexa's favorites.

For the next hour they enthusiastically ate their way through the flaky pastries—*tiropites* stuffed with cheese and *spanikopites* stuffed with spinach—followed by *souvlaki* and *moussaka*. They barely hesitated over their Greek coffees before going on to *baklava*, a dessert pastry filled with nuts and honey.

"No one in England or America has the slightest idea how good *baklava* can be. Even if they've eaten it there," Alexa declared, and with his mouth full Mark could only nod in agreement.

"Do you suppose we're making pigs of ourselves?" she asked. "Is that why we're attracting so much attention?"

"You know better," Mark said. "They're staring because we live together in your grandfather's house."

Alexa tried not to blush. "I guess you're right. Sophie said there would be gossip but that I probably wouldn't be totally ostracized since I'm an American and only half Greek."

"Well, that's a relief," Mark said jokingly.

"Be serious, Mark. It was a consideration when I was deciding whether or not you could live there—what people would think, I mean—but Sophie said nothing mattered except what I thought."

"And you thought I was harmless."

"Not exactly," she said, equivocating because she didn't want to answer his question. He wasn't harmless, and she knew it. She also knew that he wouldn't take advantage of her unless she encouraged him.

"Well, our situation is a little unusual because, let's face it, I'm a hired hand."

Alexa wasn't sure where this conversation was going, but she suddenly felt reckless and adventuresome—at dinner with a man who was different from anyone she'd ever known, more worldly and by far more handsome. No, they were well past the employer and employee stage now. "You're much more than that, Mark. You're a friend, someone who helped me out when I needed it. I owe you a great deal."

He reached across the table and touched her hand. "No, Alexa, you don't owe me a thing."

Alexa didn't move. She liked the feeling of his large, warm hand covering hers. Their eyes met and held. She couldn't look away and she couldn't stop smiling at him.

They might have sat there like that all night if the music hadn't begun. "Oh, look, Vassili is going to dance," Alexa said, relieved to be able to force her eyes away from Mark's face.

Vassili had risen from a chair in the corner where he'd been sitting with his cronies and had begun to move to the rhythm of the music, extending his arms to shoulder level and snapping his fingers, slowly, sensuously and then more quickly as the music livened and his feet began to fly.

"*Opa!*" the crowd shouted, "*Opa,* Vassili!"

"It's called the eagle," Mark said, and Alexa remembered her grandfather moving to the rhythm of that dance, appropriately named because it began in such a stately manner.

Soon, as the cheers became louder, others joined in the dance, and Alexa and Mark got to their feet, clapping along with the rest.

"They'll be smashing plates before long," Mark said over the noise, and he was right. Somewhere in the taverna, the china began to break as Niko looked on, totting up the cost in his head, and Mark and Alexa stood watching the phenomenon they'd both seen before but which still didn't fail to amaze them.

"I must say the Greeks show their pleasure in strange ways," Mark said. "Breaking plates isn't my idea of fun, but dancing," he went on, taking Alexa's arm, "that's another matter."

Everyone in the taverna had joined in the dancing, arms linked, legs kicking. Alexa vaguely remembered the dances from her childhood, and Mark must have learned them along the way, for they picked up the steps immediately. They didn't stop until it was over and the musicians, more exhausted than the dancers, had taken a break and headed for drinks at the bar.

Damp and out of breath, Alexa and Mark walked out into the night air and soon found themselves on the beach at the water's edge. Mark's arm was still around her, his drenched body pressed next to hers. He hadn't quite caught his breath.

"What a workout. It's more exhausting than putting on a roof," he said.

"And much more fun," Alexa reminded him.

"Yes," he agreed, stopping to look down at her in the wandering strip of moonlight that seemed to illuminate only their two figures in the night.

Mark turned her slowly in his arms. "I'm glad I'm here," he said. "At this moment I can't think of anywhere else I'd rather be."

He held her closer, and Alexa tilted her head back to look up at him. She could feel the sea breeze on her still-damp skin, hear the ripple of the waves, the uneven pounding of her heart. She closed her eyes, knowing he was going to kiss her.

Mark leaned forward, his lips close, so close that their breaths mingled. Then something made him pause. He didn't know quite what it was, but it had to do with guilt and integrity. It was puzzling, but he knew that he was going to back off and not kiss the woman he'd wanted to kiss so desperately for so long.

When he drew away and spoke to her, his voice was barely audible. "Let's go order our coffee and watch the end of the dancing."

Alexa didn't understand what had happened and she found herself suddenly embarrassed for wanting the kiss that never came. He couldn't have known her feelings, though, so she tried to hide the embarrassment with conversation.

The words came out stilted and made her feel so shy suddenly that she stopped talking, and as they reached the taverna she was glad to see the dancing was still going on. It gave her time to catch her breath and regain some semblance of control over her emotions.

By the time the dancing ended and their coffee was drunk and another cup ordered, everything was back to normal between her and Mark, but Alexa couldn't help feeling a little sadness. They'd been so close for a moment, and now they were back to being buddies and partners.

"Vassili's quite a dancer, isn't he?" Mark asked as the old man passed by them with a hearty greeting. "Especially for a seventy-year-old."

"But he's strong and healthy from living the good life here on Kavos."

"It's a good life now," Mark responded, "but there was a time during the war... You know I asked Vassili about it, but he never really answered me, not directly, anyway."

"Pappous was the same," Alexa told him. "He never opened up. Sometimes I—" Then she stopped. There were those half-remembered, whispered conversations she'd overheard when Pappous and her father talked about the war years and the German occupation of Kavos and the stories that had circulated then that Pappous always said were only rumors. Yet sometimes he'd talk about how easy it had been to fool the Nazis, and that had made her wonder whether or not there was a modicum of truth in the tales she'd heard.

"Sometimes you what?" Mark asked. He was stirring his coffee casually, looking out to sea, but there was something about the way he held his body that let Alexa know the question was serious. She had no answer for it.

"Oh, nothing," she admitted. "I was just thinking about my grandfather. He was a rather quixotic man."

"No more so than his granddaughter," Mark noted, looking into her eyes.

The questions ended, and the glow that had been between them on the beach seemed to return.

"No more so than you," she said.

"Then that gives us a kind of kinship, doesn't it?" It was a question that demanded no answer. It just lingered in the air with their smiles and their good feelings, staying with them on the walk home and when he kissed her cheek lightly at the bedroom door.

It wasn't a real kiss, but it was so much more than what had come in the past that Alexa cherished it even as she softly moved away into her room and closed the door between them.

She undressed quickly and then lay down on the bed, letting her confusion rise to the surface. She'd managed to hold it down all evening, but now she didn't bother. The moment that she'd somehow always known would happen between them had come and gone so quickly neither of them had had time to hold onto it—maybe Mark hadn't wanted to. Or maybe he was, like Alexa, just too unsure.

Whatever the reason, it was for the best she decided. Mark was a drifter, and although she'd also led that sort of life, it was over now. She had a chance now to make something of herself. Mark would drift on, but Alexa would stay and she would accomplish her goals.

Mark rolled over for the hundredth time, trying to get comfortable. He'd moved his mattress onto the flat part of the roof above the kitchen, thinking that the soft breeze on the night air would help him sleep. It didn't. He couldn't stop thinking about Alexa, wondering what he was going to do about her.

Finding no answer and still wide awake, he sat up. In the moonlight he could see the olive trees—twisted, silvery silhouettes. He could hear the usually restful sounds of night. But tonight he didn't relax—the sounds made him even more agitated.

Finally he got up, thinking he would go downstairs and get something to drink.

Mark went down the steps as quietly as possible, trying to avoid the two or three squeaking stairs that he was familiar with by now. He headed for the kitchen where he poured himself a glass of milk. He sat down at the table and drank it slowly, trying without success to relax. It was no use. Maybe a walk would help.

As Mark started to open the doors to the garden, he saw a flash of white. Quickly he moved into the shadows and pulled the curtains back.

The vision was gone. At least it was out of his line of sight. Slowly, inch by inch, he opened the door and stepped outside. He could see nothing. He stopped and listened. He could hear nothing. At least at first. Then there was a faint sound as if someone were moving along the walk.

Alexa was standing by the wall at the far end of the garden. The breeze caught in her hair and blew it across her forehead. She reached up with one hand to smooth it back, and the gesture was so innocent that it took Mark's breath away. He knew he should turn and walk back into the house, but he didn't. He moved toward her instead.

She was wearing a white cotton gown that clung softly to her curves, and she was barefooted. One hand still rested on the wall, and she dropped the other away from her hair, letting it fall across her eyes, where it gleamed like an ebony curtain. Her lips were parted, and she moistened them with the tip of her tongue.

Mark felt his knees grow weak as he watched. The look on Alexa's face was expectant. He moved toward her, thinking that she could be a goddess, bathed in the light of the moon, radiating a quality that was fundamental and primeval.

"Alexa." He spoke her name and reached out to touch her face. Her skin was silky beneath his fingertips. He caressed her chin and let his fingers trail across her shoulder. She was as beautiful as a Greek statue, but there was nothing of cold marble about her—Alexa was warm and inviting, soft, waiting.

Yet she wasn't really waiting, either, she was moving slowly toward him.

Mark reached out and took her hand, and then she was in his arms, her body fitting perfectly within his. For a long moment he just held her, knowing at last how it felt to have Alexa in his arms. It felt wonderful. At the harbor hours before, he had almost kissed her and then had moved away, feeling guilty. His conscience had gotten in the way then. Now he felt no pangs of guilt. He wanted to kiss her, and he *would* kiss her.

Her soft, curved lips were only a millimeter away. He touched them with his own, lightly at first, and when he felt her mouth opening to him, he pulled her closer and put the passion he felt into the kiss.

For Alexa it had all been like a dream, seeing Mark walk toward her. Now it was very real. His arms were hard and strong. She could hear the beating of his heart and the rush of his breath. His tongue touched hers, once, twice, and then invaded the recesses of her mouth.

Alexa tightened her arms around his neck, ran her hands through his thick hair as her breasts pushed against his broad chest and her hips fitted against his.

The cool breeze continued to blow, and on the night air were sounds of insects, birds and distant animals. Alexa heard none of that. She was aware only of her breath and his, felt only his lips on her mouth, her chin, her cheek and brow. She was surrounded by him, enveloped in him, and she ached with desire for him.

"Alexa..." Mark broke away, looking down at her.

He'd just said one word. He hadn't meant it to be a question, and yet maybe he had. Her response had been in answer to the question, and it had meant she was ready for him, as ready as he was for her.

No! That time he didn't speak aloud, but the denial was real. He mustn't use her. He must be fair, Mark realized as he started to turn away.

But when he looked again she was smiling at him. It was a smile he'd never seen before, an archaic smile that reminded him of nothing more than the expression of women in ancient Greek statuary. It was, like Alexa, irresistible.

Chapter 5

Alexa hadn't moved. This time Mark knew that she really was waiting for him to act. He wanted more than kisses, and so did she, Mark was sure. Maybe a stronger man could have walked away, being cruel only to be kind, but at that moment Mark wasn't strong at all.

He held out his hand. She did the same, and the moment their fingertips touched, Mark knew it was too late to turn back. He reached down and lifted her into his arms, and a little gasp escaped his lips. He hadn't expected her to be so light. She seemed almost weightless, like some kind of vision. But she wasn't a vision—she was real. The strength of her arms around his neck told Mark that.

He crossed the garden quickly, kicked open the French doors, went through the living room and down the hall, moving effortlessly as if he were carrying an angel in his arms. And he was, Mark thought.

He reached out to touch her hair and then slipped his hand down to her neck where it rested gently. "You're beautiful, Alexa," he said huskily. "I want you very much. I can't deny that now."

Alexa took a deep breath but didn't answer or try to understand the meaning of his words—she just reached for him.

Their first kiss in her bed was a hungry, searching exploration that went on and on. During the kiss, without moving his lips from hers, Mark slipped the straps of her gown off her shoulders and touched the soft rise of her breasts with unsteady hands.

He remembered how she'd looked in her dress tonight, so beautiful that every head in the taverna had turned toward them as they walked to their table. Mark was used to having his women admired by other men. It had always made him rather proud. But tonight he'd felt a sudden jealousy that others were able to see her with eyes as admiring as his own. He'd wanted her then, and the wait had only heightened his need.

He slipped the straps off her arms and then with eager hands, no longer careful, pulled down the front to expose her bare breasts. "So beautiful," he said, or tried to say. The words caught in his throat.

Alexa had felt a fire raging inside her from the moment Mark had held out his hand in the garden, for that was the moment when she knew that they would be lovers. Now, as the time drew closer and the flames grew stronger, Alexa could feel heat radiating through her body.

Then Mark reached out and touched her breasts, and it was as if his touch had ignited all of her senses. She moaned softly as he caressed her, moving his hands over the tender fullness of her breasts and below to her waist, pulling the gown down her body and tossing it carelessly onto the floor.

Everywhere he touched her, Alexa felt the heat of his hands. Her skin tingled as if her veins ran with liquid fire.

"Oh, Alexa, we should have done this long ago," Mark whispered as he pulled her body against his. He'd managed to take off his shorts so that the length of his body, warm from the summer night, damp with heat and passion, pressed against her.

Alexa could feel the night breeze through the window. It fluttered the curtains and brushed her bare skin just before his hands began their explorations anew, and the breeze was forgotten. He seemed to be memorizing her body with his hands, and each place they touched turned to fire beneath his fingers.

Then his mouth traced the pattern that his hands had discovered, and when he cupped one breast and leaned over to take the nipple in his hot, wet mouth, the fire centered below in one place, where her need was greatest. As his lips continued to work their wonders, his hands played over her body until they found that very place.

Alexa gave another gasp of pleasure as his fingers tantalized her, sliding in and out of her moistness. At the same time Mark moved his lips from her breast up the long, slim column of her neck and found her mouth, lightly kissing first her upper lip, then her lower, then each corner and finally sliding his tongue easily into her mouth, touching hers, withdrawing and then touching again, repeating the movement of his fingers with his tongue and starting another fire within her.

Instinctively Alexa reached for him, stroking lovingly along the silky hardness of his arousal, which grew larger with each movement of her hands.

"This is the way it ought to be between us," he murmured. "This is the way it should have been all along."

"I know," Alexa answered, and it was true. There seemed to be no reason for them to be apart and every reason to be together. They belonged like this, perfect, wrapped in each other's arms, bodies meshed in perfect harmony.

"If only you knew how it feels when you touch me, hold me like that," Mark said, his voice husky with need, his breath rasping in his throat. "Does this feel good, what I'm doing to you?" he asked lovingly.

"Oh, yes, my darling, Mark. Oh, yes." Her cry became a little whimper of pleasure.

"Soon it'll be even better," he whispered, "when you're ready for me."

He kissed her once more before sliding easily and gently inside her. Yes, he thought, she was ready for him, so ready and so welcoming.

For a moment they both relaxed, delighted with the feeling of being together at last, of his hard strength inside her softness. But the moment was over quickly as their dual passion guided them into a mindless glory of lovemaking in which there was no rationality—only feelings, emotions, desires expressed and satisfied as Mark moved within Alexa, filling her with his love.

She arched upward to meet each thrust, accepting that love and giving in return all the deep feelings she possessed.

Each time he filled her and then withdrew and then filled her again, Alexa lost control of herself. She cried out in ecstasy, sure that the next time would never equal what she was feeling. Then it happened again, the deep spiraling sensation that shook her to her very soul. Just when she believed the end was coming, Mark held back, waiting, leaving her on the brink before letting her go over at last with an all-consuming explosion unlike anything she'd ever experienced.

She tried to call his name, but she never knew if the word had escaped her throat or not. It seemed like hours later before reality descended on her, leaving her damp and spent, stretched across the bed, wrapped in his arms and legs.

"You're beautiful," he said when those hours, real or imagined, had passed. "But I've always known that. You're also desirable, more desirable than anyone. And I didn't know that. Although I suspected," he added with a grin Alexa didn't see, for her eyes were closed as she snuggled next to him.

The next morning, when Mark woke up, Alexa was still sleeping, her legs entwined in his and one arm thrown across his shoulder. For a while he just lay there and watched her sleep. Her mouth was slightly open, and she made the most adorable noise, a sort of whisper but without words. He could have lain there all morning looking at her, but Mark knew there was work to do, and besides, he wanted to have her breakfast ready when she woke up. So he kissed her lightly on the top of her head, disengaged himself carefully and got up, pulling on his shorts as he headed for the kitchen.

With the light of day, Mark knew he had to face what had happened and how it would seem to an outsider. Anyone would think he'd taken advantage of her, and under any other circumstances, with any other woman, they might have been right. But not this time, and not with Alexa.

Yet he knew that was how it would look. Dammit, he thought to himself, he didn't care how it *looked*. All that mattered was how it felt, and it felt good, being with Alexa. Just as he'd told her, it felt right for them to be lovers. There was no other way it could have happened, he argued inwardly. It had to be.

When Alexa finally came into the kitchen, she was shy—Mark could tell that by the way she walked through the door, not looking at him but smiling that archaic Greek goddess smile.

Mark waited for her to speak, but the wait was very long, almost awkward, and still she was silent. Finally he jumped in, hoping to relieve her shyness.

Moving away from the stove he took her in his arms and kissed her hungrily, hugging her and holding her close. "I missed you," he said.

"Missed me?"

"Yes, I've been up an hour, and I missed you every minute of it. Do you realize," he said with mock seriousness, "that we've been together, living in the same house, for almost two weeks?"

"Two weeks and a day, actually," she said, adding with a laugh, "I guess you passed your probation."

"Never mind that," Mark said. "My question is, have you been wanting what I've been wanting during that time?"

She shook her head. "Only for part of it. The greatest part," she added, and they both laughed.

She breathed a sigh of relief. The ice was broken; they were going to be all right. Alexa had dreaded this time, coming down to breakfast as usual but with everything different between them. She'd been unsure, shy, wondering how Mark would react to her, worried about the awkwardness they both might feel. But it had only lasted a moment, and now it was over. She'd gotten through it, they'd gotten through it, with laughter. It was amazing, she thought, what a large part laughter had in their relationship. This morning it made everything so easy.

"What's for breakfast?" Alexa asked.

"Lots of things. Toast, marmalade, fruit, sausage, bacon, eggs—"

"Mark, do you think all of that is necessary?"

"Absolutely. We have a long, hard day ahead of us and," he said with a grin, "a long, easy night." He kissed her quickly and led her to the table.

Alexa had just taken her first bite when she heard the knock at the front gate. "Who in the world could it be at this hour?"

Mark laughed. "Look at the clock, sleepyhead. It's almost ten."

"Well, just the same, I wonder who it could be." Alexa started to get up, but Mark motioned her back. "Go ahead and finish your breakfast. I'll go to the gate. It's probably Vassili."

"He'd come on in, and so would Sophie," Alexa answered as Mark disappeared into the courtyard. With a shrug, she started on her breakfast, surprised at her hunger. Mark was right. He seemed to know her better than she knew herself, and for some reason that made Alexa very happy. In fact she hadn't felt as good about her life in a very long time.

A smattering of conversation drifted back to her from the courtyard, and Alexa determined that there were two visitors, a man and a woman. She didn't recognize either voice and continued her meal until a possibility crept into her mind. They could be tourists, visitors to the island looking for a place to stay.

Obviously they couldn't stay here. She was nowhere near ready to take in guests, but she certainly could make them welcome. After all, they might come back next season or recommend Villa Alexi to their friends.

Quickly Alexa gulped down her coffee and headed for the courtyard. She could tell that she'd guessed correctly about the voices. They came from tourists, all right, a man and a woman, well dressed and looking very wealthy indeed.

Alexa sized up the couple as she approached. The woman was in her early thirties, tall and slim. Her red hair was cut very short, and her white slacks and blouse showed off an even, hard-earned tan. The man was about her height, stockier in build with brown hair and a mustache. They seemed very much at ease with each other, and yet Alexa couldn't help but think that there was something strange about their relationship.

She shrugged off her feelings, trying to imagine how Mark would chastise her later, telling her that no one could possibly judge what was happening between a man and a woman before even saying hello to them, and no doubt he would be right. And yet . . .

Mark, obviously unaware of her thoughts, introduced her. "Alexa, this is Tony and Charlotte Whitfield. They've been admiring your house from the distance."

The couple shook Alexa's hand and gushed about the house, the beauty of the setting and the view in a way that was terribly un-English, although English was certainly what they were. In fact, their accents were very, very upper-class Brit, Alexa decided. Despite that, they were far from reserved.

"We've been cruising the Aegean, and this is our first visit to Kavos," Charlotte said. "We know absolutely nothing about it, but this house seemed to personify the island for us. Imagine our surprise," she added, "when we found one of our countrymen here and an owner who's American!"

"Would you like to look around?" Alexa asked. "We're remodeling, but—"

"So Mark told us," Tony interrupted with continued enthusiasm, "and we'd love to see the house if you don't mind. As a matter of fact, we've been looking for an investment."

It was Alexa's turn to interrupt. "I'm not remodeling in order to sell the house. I plan to turn it into a hotel."

"Really?"

Alexa thought Charlotte's response was a little disbelieving, but she tried not to notice. She *was* going to open a hotel eventually. "Yes," she said firmly. "But you and your husband are welcome to have a look anyway. After all, I might get you back as guests someday."

Tony laughed. "Indeed you might. And by the way, Alexa, Charlotte is my sister, not my wife."

"Oh, I'm sorry," Alexa sputtered. That explained her earlier feeling about the relationship, she decided, although something about it still seemed a little strange to her.

"Oh, it's quite all right," Charlotte said. "People often make that mistake."

They began the tour at the entranceway to the house, and as they passed through each room, Charlotte and Tony became more enthusiastic. It was true, Alexa thought, that the house was coming along nicely. She felt rather proud of the progress she and Mark had made and happy to hear the visitors' praise. After all, these were the first tourists to see Villa Alexi.

And she liked them very much, Alexa decided by the time they had completed the tour and settled in the kitchen for coffee.

"I still haven't quite mastered this skill," Alexa admitted as she set the cups of coffee before her guests.

"I'm sure it's quite good," Charlotte said, reaching for a spoon.

"No, don't stir," Tony reminded her as Alexa and Mark sat back with smiles, letting him teach his sister the correct way to drink a cup of Greek coffee.

"Oh, I remember now," Charlotte said. "The grounds are left in the mixture, and I must let them sink to the bottom and then drink the coffee off the top." She took a sip. "And I might add that's a good idea," she said after a slight gasp. "It's certainly strong enough without stirring."

"I agree," Alexa said. "When I had my first cup of Greek coffee I think I stayed awake for days. Now I'm beginning to get used to it, but I certainly understand why they use such small cups!"

They lingered in the kitchen for the better part of an hour, talking about Greece and the idiosyncracies of its people, their charm and their humor. Although the Whitfields' manner had seemed a little forced to Alexa at first, the more she talked to them, the better Alexa liked the brother and sister.

Mark didn't seem to share her sentiments. He'd grown strangely quiet and at one point, when Tony asked about his work, leaned back in his chair, crossed his arms and answered, "I'm just the handyman here."

Alexa frowned at Mark, barely resisting the urge to kick him under the table, and quickly informed Charlotte and Tony of his scholarly background. "He's on a sabbatical here—kind of."

Charlotte was quick to help smooth things over. "And like many of us English," she said, "captivated by the islands."

At the Whitfields' insistence, Alexa told them about her association with Greece and the island of Kavos. Soon she launched into the story of her inheritance and its accompanying problems. The pair listened intently, asking the right questions and commiserating when she told them of her disappointments. Clearly they were fascinated by her spirit of adventure.

By the time they were ready to leave, Alexa was enjoying herself thoroughly and was charmed by the invitation to visit their yacht anchored in the harbor.

"We plan to be here for a while so you must join us for dinner," Tony insisted.

Not until they'd gone did Mark make his feelings known, and then only when Alexa prodded.

"What's the matter, Mark? Why were you so unfriendly?"

"Maybe I just wanted to be alone with you this morning. Can you blame me?" he asked slyly, coming up behind Alexa and slipping his arms around her waist.

"No, because I had the same feeling." Alexa leaned back against him as his lips tickled her neck.

"Well, you didn't show it, the way you acted with them—like they were your long-lost friends. And if I sound jealous, hell, it's because I am."

Alexa smiled. "I guess I did go on a little too long, but I liked them, in an odd sort of way. They're ... different."

"You can say that again."

"And I would enjoy going on the yacht," Alexa continued, turning to give him a kiss before she moved away.

"You said yourself we didn't have time for that sort of thing, Alexa. There was barely time for dinner at the taverna. We have too much work, remember?"

"I know, but the yacht sounds so tempting."

"Which, I imagine, is just the response Tony was hoping for."

"What in the world does that mean?" Alexa had begun clearing away the coffee cups and stopped while she tried to analyze his remark.

"It means Tony couldn't keep his eyes off you."

"That's ridiculous, Mark. He's just very nice, and so is his sister."

"Sister?" Mark shook his head. "She's no more his sister than I am."

"Then why did he—"

"I don't know, Alexa, but as you say, it's all very odd. Don't you wonder why they just happened to turn up on your doorstep?"

Alexa put her cup on the kitchen counter and sat back down beside Mark. "Because they liked the house," she said thoughtfully, almost doubting the validity of her response.

"Sure, Alexa," Mark answered sarcastically. "They were just standing around by the harbor and said to each other, 'Oh, let's follow this road and see if we like the house at the end of it.' Alexa, you can't even *see* this house until you're almost in the front yard."

"Well, they could have stumbled upon it. That happens. Anyway, I'm not going to make a mystery out of something so silly. We probably won't hear from them again, so let's get to work."

Alexa was wrong; they heard from the Whitfields shortly before dark when one of the boys from the taverna delivered a note, handwritten on engraved stationery.

"It's not an invitation to dinner at all," she told Mark. "They want us to join them in the morning for a sailing trip up north. Oh, Mark, let's go, please. I've just been dying to see those ruins again. I haven't been to that part of the island since I was a child."

Mark couldn't help smiling. She'd even begun to sound like a child the way she bubbled with excitement. But he was wary. Mark knew from past experience to trust his first impressions, which in this case weren't good at all. On the other hand, he didn't want to alarm Alexa.

"I don't know. There really is a great deal of work to do tomorrow."

"Oh, Mark, don't spoil this. It's the only chance I've had to see the ruins."

"Well, of course you could go with them while I stay here and work on—"

Alexa interrupted immediately. "No, I wouldn't want to go without you."

As soon as she'd spoken the words, she realized how they sounded, and so did he. "And I wouldn't want you to," he said, reaching across the table to take her hand. "Besides, it could be pretty romantic on a sailboat with you. If the Whitfields would be good sports and stay below deck."

Alexa laughed. "Then you'll go?"

"I'll go," Mark said, but he couldn't share her excitement.

The Whitfields didn't wait for Mark and Alexa to meet them at the harbor the next morning. They climbed the hill and were rapping on the door just after seven o'clock.

"I'm glad we managed to roll out of bed early," Mark said when he heard the knock, "or they might have interrupted something very special." He came out of the bathroom in his robe, his face still covered with shaving cream. "As it is, they've only managed to interrupt this." He reached out and grabbed Alexa as she headed out the bedroom door, giving her a big kiss that left lather all over the side of her face.

"Mark!" She looked in the mirror at her reflection. "Coming," she called loudly before running into the bathroom, wiping off the cream with Mark's washcloth and then running back past him and down the hall, trying to keep from laughing.

"I hope we're not too early," Tony said when she greeted them. "But Charlotte couldn't wait for you to join us. Just had to come up and get you. I think she wanted another look at the house."

"You're probably right, and do you blame me? This is my favorite spot in Greece," Charlotte declared.

"Oh, what a compliment," Alexa said as she led the couple through the house, out the back door and into the garden, thinking to herself how beautiful it was and how perfect it would be when Villa Alexi became a reality.

"If you don't mind waiting here, I'll run in and get my things."

"Where's Mark?"

"Well, he's, he's... I'm sure he'll be right out," she finally managed, not answering the question at all.

"Don't let Charlotte rush you," Tony said. "It's so pleasant out here we probably could be persuaded to stay."

"Oh, no, you don't," Alexa answered with a laugh. "I'm not about to give up my chance to go sailing with you." She was really getting along fine with the Whitfields, Alexa thought, and Mark was wrong. This was going to be a beautiful day.

* * *

By noon they'd sailed almost halfway around the island to a point where the hills ended in steep, rocky cliffs. At the bottom of the cliffs was a crescent beach, several hundred feet below the remains of a temple to Apollo, which consisted of four columns set against the bright blue sky. Alexa hadn't seen the ruins since her childhood—they took her breath away.

As they anchored in the harbor and the men let down the dinghy, she could hardly contain herself. "This time I'm going to climb up there," she said. "Pappous never would let me. 'Too dangerous for a little girl,' he always said. But I'm not a little girl anymore."

Mark laughed and shook his head in amazement. She certainly wasn't a little girl. In fact, she was more woman than anyone he'd ever known, and more adventurous than he'd ever suspected. "I'm with you," he said, hoping to steal some time alone with Alexa.

They'd all piled into the dinghy and headed for shore, Charlotte listening in amazement to their conversation. "I can't believe you actually plan to go up there, Alexa. We just came for the view, didn't we, Tony?"

Squinting against the bright sunlight, Tony looked up at the temple. "Actually I rather fancy the idea of a climb. See what it looks like from close up."

"Just exactly what it looks like from far away," Charlotte decided, "but much less safe. Alexa, you stay here with me and let the men climb."

"Nope," Alexa declared cheerily as they approached the rocky beach and Mark jumped out to pull the dinghy ashore. "I'm going up there."

She did, but it wasn't as easy a task as she had supposed. Charlotte, once she'd accepted the fact that Alexa really was going to climb, became a one-woman cheering squad, encouraging her to make it to the top before the men.

Alexa just hoped to make it, period. Carefully, step by step, she followed Mark, placing each foot into the space he'd made for her while Tony brought up the rear, whistling happily.

"It's just like the romp they used to put us through when I was a kid in school," he told them. " 'Makes a man of you,' they declared then, and all I can remember is wishing I were back in my warm bed. This time I'm going to enjoy the challenge. I think," he added as his foot slipped and he barely caught himself by grabbing the branch of a shrub.

Mark reached past Alexa and got a good grip on Tony's arm. "No more talking, Tony," he advised, "so you can pay attention to your footing."

"Whatever you say, my dear guide," Tony answered lightly, as he inched his foot carefully into a safe haven and released his grasp on the spindly shrub.

Step by step, they reached the level path where the going was easier and they could finally stop to take a breather.

Alexa looked around, spellbound. The view from so near the top was more spectacular than she'd imagined. Suddenly she was anxious to go on, to reach the pinnacle where Apollo's temple was poised.

Mark had to stop Alexa from running the last few yards. "It's more dangerous than it looks," he reminded her. "Don't hurry. Sometimes it's good to take things slow and easy." His hand touched her cheek, and she saw in his eyes the same glow she'd seen that morning in bed.

"Sometimes," she teased, "and sometimes reckless abandon is best."

But Alexa did as he suggested, waiting for Mark and Tony to catch up before she continued along the path that hugged the edge of the cliff, not stopping until she had to, when only sheer rock remained between her and her destination.

Impatiently Alexa waited for Mark so that he could go ahead and then pull each of them up the rock to the level ground above.

Then they were there, surrounded by a brilliant blue sky that rushed downward to an equally blue sea, the whole effect like a vault around them. It was broken only by occasional whitecaps out to sea, purple smudges of distant islands and, towering above them, the stark columns of Apollo's temple, pure and majestic.

They all stood speechless for a time before regaining their breath and their senses as Tony attempted to define the beauty of the view.

"It's like a picture postcard," he decided.

"I feel so small," Alexa observed as she made her way to the remains of Apollo's temple. "How could they ever have constructed anything here?"

"Or on any other acropolis in Greece," Mark responded. "The height itself is enough to boggle the modern mind."

Alexa had moved ahead to the columns, where wildflowers grew in profusion, entwining themselves around the marble bases and throughout the fluted ruins that lay on the ground. From the hills the sweet smell of pine wafted on the breeze. Alexa had never felt so much one with Greece as she felt at that moment.

Mark, seeing her reaction, was careful to leave her to her thoughts, and Alexa appreciated that.

Tony was another matter. With every step she took, every turn and every pause, Tony was beside her, adding his comments to her thoughts, advising her, looking after her.

"Let me give you a hand, Alexa," he said as she scrambled over a fallen column in an effort to get a better perspective. "I wouldn't want you to scrape those pretty knees in a fall."

Later, when they were almost ready to make their descent, he was there again, urging her to stay a little longer.

"Charlotte will have our lunch out by now," Alexa objected, aware that she would have liked nothing better than to linger for hours, but unwilling to have Tony as her constant companion, and obviously Tony wasn't going to leave her alone with Mark. "We should start down."

Tony objected again, and throughout their dialogue Mark remained silent, watching Tony with a look that Alexa was unable to interpret. Finally they all agreed that the time had come to leave the temple of Apollo and get back down to earth and reality.

Charlotte was waiting with their lunch of cold grilled chicken, pâtés and salad, which Alexa realized must have come not from the taverna but from the chef on the Whitfields' yacht.

Mark decided to go for a swim before lunch, and Tony followed after unsuccessfully urging Alexa to join them. She'd had enough exercise for the day, Alexa declared, uneasy over Tony's attentions as she'd been all day.

Just as bothersome were Charlotte's references to Mark who, Alexa had to admit, didn't help matters at all when he stripped down to his bathing suit, revealing a body that was taut and tanned and greatly admired by Charlotte.

"Have you known him long?" she asked Alexa pointedly.

"Only since he came to work for me," Alexa responded, noting that Charlotte's interest in Mark was as great as Tony's interest in her. In a more jaded moment, she might have agreed with Mark that the two were not brother and sister but husband and wife, looking for a romantic fling on their holiday. On the other hand, if they were siblings as they professed, they seemed to be locked in competition to see who would gain the favor of Alexa and Mark first.

The whole situation was beginning to confuse Alexa terribly, but she still couldn't hide her interest in the Whitfields. In spite of Tony's unwanted attention and Charlotte's curiosity, they were a likable pair, whatever their relationship.

"It must be interesting," Charlotte was commenting, "with the two of you living alone in that house."

"It's a big house," Alexa reminded her. "And it was beneficial to our financial situation for him to move in." Alexa thought of the past two nights, sleeping next to Mark, reaching out for him, making love to him, and she struggled diligently to keep her voice matter-of-fact.

"Hmm," Charlotte observed as Alexa tried to avoid a look that might be misinterpreted. If she and Charlotte had known each other longer, been closer, she might have been tempted to tell her everything, but she managed to restrain herself. After all, Charlotte—and Tony—were still enigmas to her.

"Well, it's rather exciting," Charlotte went on, "living with a stranger, a man you know nothing about."

"I know more about him than I know about you and Tony, and yet I doubt if you have any deep, dark secrets. Or am I wrong?" Alexa was pleased she'd been able to turn the conversation away from her and Mark.

"Oh, darling, I wish we did have a secret. Unfortunately we're just two boring Brits sailing around the Aegean, happy to meet some people full of energy and fun."

"And I for one am glad you and Tony landed on Kavos," Alexa said.

That feeling lingered as the men joined them, shaking water from their hair and drying off with towels Charlotte supplied before settling down to lunch. Even the talk after they'd eaten and stretched out on the beach towels in the sun didn't completely dampen Alexa's spirits.

She didn't know who brought it up, Mark or Tony, but before she realized it the war was the subject of conversation.

"They had a tough time back then," Tony was saying, "not just on the mainland but in the islands, too."

"It was lucky, wasn't it," Charlotte added, "how many of the historical sites were preserved."

"That didn't stop the Nazis from making off with all kinds of treasure," Tony said. "I imagine there are still quite a few hidden, buried—"

"Or so the story goes," Mark said lazily. He didn't seem to be interested in the subject, and yet Alexa had the feeling that he'd been the one who'd brought it up.

"Surely you've heard all the rumors," Charlotte persisted.

"I never listen to rumors," Mark said, reaching for his shirt.

"What about you, Alexa?" Charlotte went on.

"I'd love to find a treasure," she answered, opening her eyes wide.

Mark pulled on his shirt and took a beer out of the cooler. "The biggest theft was when Lord Elgin took a piece of the Parthenon back to England about a hundred and fifty years ago," he said wryly.

"Oh, no, not the Elgin Marbles argument again," Charlotte groaned.

"We've kept them safe," Tony maintained, "right there in the British Museum. No smog, no pollution."

"Safe and all yours," Mark pointed out.

"Wait a minute, old boy," Tony said. "You're a British citizen, too."

"But not always a loyal one," Mark said cynically, "especially on this subject."

Alexa chimed in then. "As a minority, a Yank among you Brits, I'd say the marbles deserve to be back on the Acropolis."

Mark was leaning back against the dinghy, his shirt stretched tight over his chest, his blond hair gleaming in the sun and his eyes as blue as the sea. "So you'd be in favor of the world's museums sending their treasures back to Greece?" he asked Alexa pointedly.

"Why not?" she responded grandly.

He smiled. "I think you have a good point, but you may get a dispute from our friends here."

"There's nothing wrong with a little difference of opinion, is there?" she asked the other three at large.

"Certainly not," Tony answered, "as long as it's theoretical."

"What else would it be?" Alexa asked as she leaned back beside Mark, missing the look that passed between Tony and Charlotte.

Chapter 6

They sailed into the harbor at sunset. The sky was turning bright orange with fringes of purple along the horizon, and Alexa, as always when the colors of Greece were spread as if on a palette before her, was spellbound. Mark moved to the bow of the sailboat near her. Once more he seemed to know just how she felt and was silent as he moved closer. Their shoulders touched, and for a brief moment he held her hand and then released it as Tony approached.

The man was ever the pest, Mark thought, stepping a little away from Alexa.

"Another beautiful sight," Charlotte said softly as she joined them.

Mark smiled in agreement. He'd lost his moment with Alexa, and if they couldn't be alone, why not add Charlotte to the group, he thought. At least she was less obtrusive than her "brother."

"I'm getting very fond of Kavos," Charlotte admitted.

Mark could understand that; even without Alexa on it, the island was a vacationer's paradise. With the addition of Alexa, it couldn't be surpassed. "You're right," he said as the town, brilliantly white against the horizon, grew larger at their approach. Lights were beginning to flicker on in scattered houses nestled against the hills, and the picture-postcard look of the scene was magical.

"It's getting to me, too," Tony said. "What would you think about staying a while longer, Char?"

"I'd love it."

"Who knows," Tony went on, "we might even buy a place here, it's so pleasant. And I'm not talking about an investment," he added. "I'm talking about a vacation home."

"Well, Alexa's house is out. We know that much," Charlotte reminded him.

Alexa laughed. "As of today. Ask me again in a week or two."

But she knew, if everyone else didn't, that her answer was flip. She would never give up her grandfather's house—not as long as she had the faith to believe in her goal.

As darkness fell, Alexa and Mark made their way up the narrow, winding streets toward Villa Alexi.

For the first time since the early morning, Mark put his arm around Alexa and held her close. It had been a long day for him, thinking about the night that had come before and looking forward to the one ahead.

"Alexa..."

She looked up at him, and he knew that her thoughts had also wandered back to last night. Slowly he bent and kissed her lips. "I've been wanting to do that all day," he said as she leaned against him.

"I know," she answered. "Up on the acropolis, I thought how much more wonderful it would have been if we could have..."

"Made love there among the ruins?"

"Mark! No, I was just thinking if we'd been alone how much more beautiful it would have been."

"*You* wanted to go with the Whitfields," he reminded her.

"They were our only offer," Alexa said with a laugh. "Anyway, I like them. And yet..."

"What?" Mark asked.

"Oh, I don't know. They seem to harp on the house, and I can only guess they're joking about wanting to buy it. What else could it be?" she asked almost to herself. "Even if it were on the market, it's not in shape to sell yet."

"No, it's not," Mark agreed. He seemed preoccupied, and Alexa felt the need to persist.

"I still like them," she insisted stoutly, "and if they do move here—"

"I know," Mark answered. "Others will follow." There was a smile in his voice, and Alexa realized that whatever had been bothering him moments before was in the past now.

Still, something nagged at her. "You don't like the Whitfields, do you?"

"I don't know them," he said evasively. "And even if I did, I wouldn't be inclined to give my trust and friendship so easily," he added, and Alexa realized that he was scolding her. "It might be wise for you to be a little more discerning, Alexa."

"Discerning?"

"Yes, exercise some caution," he told her as they turned the sharp corner that led up the hill to Villa Alexi.

She walked beside him, not speaking until they had reached the door, and then she turned to look at him, her hand on the gate. "If I were more cautious, I wouldn't have hired you, would I?"

Mark pushed the gate open for her, laughing. "*Touché*, Alexa. I bow to your lack of caution." Mark's lips curved into a wry grin as he followed her across the patio.

He noticed that the door to the house was open at the same moment Alexa stepped inside. He reached for her, but she was already in the kitchen. There was a split second of deafening silence before she shrieked.

She was standing in the middle of the room. All around her pots and pans had been hurled onto the floor. Food was turned out of containers. Coffee was scattered like dark sand across the tile. With a faint smothered cry, Alexa ran across the kitchen and down the hall.

This time Mark caught her, hurling her roughly back against the wall.

Alexa's breath caught in her throat, and she started to lash out at him, but he silenced her with a word.

"Quiet. Stay there and don't move. Whoever did this may still be here."

He disappeared down the hall while Alexa, more angry now than frightened, remained frozen to the spot as he'd advised.

She could hear him upstairs, going from room to room, and as she listened, Alexa remembered the look on his face when he'd pressed her against the wall, instructing her in a voice that was quiet and steady. He'd seemed so competent, so coolly professional, different from the Mark she knew. In spite of Alexa's anxiety about what had happened in her house, she couldn't get rid of that vision.

When he returned, Mark silently took her hand and led her back into the kitchen, clearing a path to the table and insisting that she sit down.

"There's no one here, but every room has been turned upside down," he told her.

"Thieves on Kavos? Who could it be?" Alexa couldn't imagine. She'd never heard of any crime on the island. And yet she was trembling at the possibility.

"I don't know," Mark answered. "Maybe it was just kids."

Alexa shook her head. "Greek parents watch their children carefully. There's no vandalism on Kavos." But as she looked around the room, she was unable to come up with any other explanation. "I guess it must be vandalism. I can't tell if anything's been taken, but it looks like they just threw it all on the floor. Are the other rooms like this?"

Mark nodded.

"How dare they?" she cried out, more angry now than ever.

"Alexa, don't." There was something in Mark's voice, as if he had a second sense that understood what was going on inside her and was trying to stem the tide of feelings, knowing where it would lead.

But it was too late. The tears had erupted in spite of her attempts to hold them back, and suddenly Alexa was reduced to helpless sobbing.

Even though he'd expected them, for a moment her tears made Mark pause, not responding, just reacting in amazement. She'd been so tough, so sure of herself even in the moments when she'd had doubts. She'd always fought back and gained control. But this had really done her in. And her vulnerability brought forth feelings in Mark that he'd thought were long gone.

He closed the space between them with one stride and took her in his arms.

"Alexa," he whispered, "it's all right. I'm here. It's all right," he repeated, holding her close, feeling a tenderness toward her that he hadn't experienced before even when they'd made love. And the need to love her now wasn't physical but emotional.

"I'm sorry," she said through her sobs.

"There's nothing wrong with being afraid," he assured her.

"I'm not really afraid," she told him, "just angry, so damned angry. I feel invaded. How dare they?" she cried out.

"Sit down, Alexa," he advised, helping her into a chair beside the kitchen table. "I'll be right back."

Mark returned from his room moments later, a brown bottle in his hand.

"Metaxa," she said. "I didn't know you had any of that."

"I was saving it for a special occasion." He smiled as he poured a little brandy into a glass. "This will just have to do."

"Well, it's special, I suppose. I've never been vandalized before." She took a sip from her glass. It went down her throat like liquid fire.

"And you never will be again," he said with a determination in his voice that soothed her.

"Oh, Mark," she said, reaching for his hand, "Thank you for being here."

"You can count on me, Alexa." He pressed her hand and realized that he meant the words. He would be here for her. But for how long? It might not be for as long as she would need him, Mark thought, but at least it would be for now, for this night. Tomorrow would come when it would come.

"Let's go to bed," he said quietly.

Without a word, Alexa stood up beside him, taking his hand.

Her room was comforting because he was there, and Alexa was willing to let him take charge. She didn't seem to have the energy to do anything. Waiting patiently, she watched as he moved across the room, turned on the light beside the bed, pulled back the covers and closed the curtains. Then, carefully and with great tenderness, he began to pick up the clothes that had been thrown out of her closet and onto the bedroom floor. He hung them up while she could only stand and watch. After he'd finished he straightened the bookshelves, replaced some of the books and continued to pick up other overturned items until the room looked fairly presentable.

"We'll get to the rest tomorrow," he told her.

"I feel helpless."

"There's nothing wrong with that," Mark answered. "We all need someone to look after us occasionally."

Alexa dropped down onto the bed. "Who looks after you, Mark?"

"No one yet," he answered. "But maybe my day will come."

For some reason Alexa couldn't imagine that it ever would. But her day certainly had. Even when she bent over to take off her sandals, Mark stopped her.

"No. I'll do that."

"Are you going to undress me, too?" she asked, almost teasingly in spite of her lack of spirit.

"Yes," he answered simply. But there was no lasciviousness in his voice or in his hands as they carefully unbuttoned her cotton shirt and slipped it off her shoulders.

Mark knew that this wasn't the time to let his desires take over. She needed comfort and reassurance, but that was all, so he managed to control his fingers as they worked with the hook on her denim skirt and then tugged at the zipper until it slid down. Alexa was able to help by standing up and stepping out of the skirt.

"I can do the rest," she said, and Mark realized that he would have to let her. If he went any further he might not be able to stem the urge to kiss the cleavage between her snowy breasts as he removed her bra or the inside of her soft yet firm thighs as he stripped off her panties.

So he moved aside and let her do the rest, trying to quiet his ragged breathing. Finally Alexa pulled on her gown and slipped into bed. Still wearing his T-shirt and chinos, Mark lay down beside her. She nestled in his arms and almost instantly fell asleep.

Somehow, and he never was quite sure how, Mark also managed to sleep that night, but his dreams weren't pleasant ones about Alexa. They were violent snatches from the past mixed with what he feared could be the very near future. He awakened from them, as he often did from unpleasant dreams, in a cold sweat.

This time Alexa was there for him. "Mark," she said, "Mark, what is it? What's the matter?" Her arms went around him automatically and she held his damp face against her.

He caught himself just before he could reach under his pillow for what he realized at the last instant wasn't there.

"Mark?" There was deep concern in Alexa's voice.

"I'm sorry, Alexa," he said. "It was just a dream."

"A nightmare, you mean." Her hands slid down his shoulders to his damp arms. "You're wet all over."

"It's like an oven in here," Mark answered as he swung his legs over the side of the bed. "And I'm still dressed." He got up and pulled off his clothes before going to the window and opening the shutters to let in a cool breeze.

Moonlight came in with the breeze, and it danced across the bed where Alexa lay, her dark hair spread out on the pillow, her fair skin shimmering for him. She wasn't afraid for herself anymore; she wasn't angry about the vandalism of her house. She was Alexa again, strong, caring, reaching out to him.

"Come to bed," she said, her voice soft, as if she'd captured some of the moonlight in it.

He took her hand.

Alexa felt herself come alive at his touch, and she pulled him toward her. Just before his lips touched hers he spoke. "You're all right now?"

"Yes," she whispered. "And you?"

"I'm fine. Just a bad dream." By the time the last word escaped his lips, Mark was kissing her, not tenderly but with the passion of the night.

Alexa responded with equal passion as he lay down beside her on the bed, his hands roaming her body— down her arms, her waist, drifting around to cup her buttocks and pull them closer as his legs enfolded her.

Alexa raised her hips slightly and in that instant they were one. It was a fierce and hungry joining. They moved together with such passion they hardly had time to kiss or caress. The power of their longing blocked out even the desire each had to give and to receive.

It happened for them at once, a shuddering, almost violent release that seemed to take them out of themselves into another part of the universe.

When it was over and they lay sated in each other's arms, Mark said softly, "I'm sorry. That was much too brief."

Alexa smiled, and because his fingers were touching her face, he could feel the corners of her mouth turn up. "Please don't be sorry," she said. "It was wonderful for me."

"I'm so glad," he answered with relief, "because it was for me, too." Then he smiled back at Alexa as he pulled her close, and once again they fell asleep, this time peacefully, each wrapped in the memory of what had happened.

* * *

When Alexa awoke the sun was also up, and another bright and beautiful island morning was upon them. Mark had already discovered the day and had chosen to turn his back on it to look at Alexa instead. He was propped on his elbow, his hair tousled, his eyes bright.

"I like this," she said.

"What?"

"Waking up beside you." There was nothing shy about Alexa's answer, nothing shy about her feelings for him.

"I like it, too," he said, leaning down to kiss her. "*Kalimera thespinis,* Alexa."

"*Kalimera*, Marco." Alexa smiled. She couldn't seem to stop smiling.

"Making love last night was certainly different for us," he said, remembering. "I wonder what it would be like if—"

"Mark, it's broad daylight," Alexa answered.

"All the better," he said, putting his arms around her and kissing her neck.

Alexa could feel his faint growth of beard against her skin, and it excited her more than she wanted to admit. "That's not what I meant," she told him. "Because it's daylight, we have to go to work." Alexa didn't want that any more than Mark did, and he knew it.

"I have an idea," he said. "Let's stay in bed all day and make love over and over until we're both satiated."

"And exhausted," she teased.

"That, too," he answered as he let his hands drift languidly down her bare neck and arms to her breasts as Alexa caught her breath.

"Oh, Mark," she said, drifting into a kiss that threatened to carry her away completely if she let it. But Alexa didn't let it; she knew better. Moving her lips away from his she reminded him, "You know how far behind we are, especially after taking a day off for the boat trip."

"I know," he answered seriously. "It was only a fantasy on my part, that day in bed. No time for fantasy today. We need to work." He kissed her again quickly and then again, lingeringly, "Hmm."

"Mark . . ."

"All right, but wait until tonight." He reached for his pants. "I'll clean up in the kitchen while you shower."

Alexa looked around the room and remembered what had happened. "Do you know that I haven't thought about the break-in since last night? Even when we woke up in the middle of the night and . . ."

"Made love," he finished for her.

"I didn't even think of it then."

"I'm glad to hear that," Mark said with a smile. "Now go and get a shower while I clean up the place. Then we'll have to report all this vandalism."

Alexa took a long shower. The water was warm and soothing, pouring down her body like cool silk, as gentle and sensuous as Mark's touch. She thought about Mark as she shampooed her hair, remembering last night and the night before. Their lovemaking hadn't been unexpected, really. She'd wanted him since that first day, but for once in her life she'd been afraid to act on her impulse.

Alexa rinsed her hair, stepped out of the shower and dried off, wondering why Mark had waited if he'd felt the same, and somehow she was sure he had. But he seemed to have been hesitant for a reason that Alexa couldn't understand.

She tried to put everything in perspective. True, they had become lovers. Yet did that change anything? Mark was still a drifter, a mysterious man who'd suddenly appeared on Kavos and might just as suddenly disappear. She had no right to expect that he would stay on when the house was finished.

Alexa stepped into a pair of shorts and for the first time began to wish that they weren't making so much progress with their work.

After breakfast they finished cleaning up the mess in the kitchen and moved on to the living room, where the damage was even more extensive.

While Mark was rehanging the curtains, Alexa began to get her desk put back together, picking up the papers that had been pulled out of the file drawer and sorting through them, trying to make some order out of the chaos.

She'd just returned everything to its proper place and was about to close the drawer when she let out a gasp of discovery. "I know what it is, Mark! I know what they took," she cried.

Mark hooked the curtain rod in place, moved to the desk and looked over Alexa's shoulders. "One of the legal documents?"

"Yes," she told them. "My grandfather's will. I kept it in the front folder of this drawer."

"Are you sure it didn't get in with some of the other papers?"

"Positive. I've gone through all of them."

Mark pushed his hands down into his pockets, looking out the window toward the sea, his thoughts seemingly a mile away. "I wonder why they would take his will?" he asked, almost to himself.

"I haven't the slightest idea. There was a letter attached to it, a personal one that means nothing to anyone but me. I told you about it," she reminded him.

He nodded. "Well, now you have something concrete to report. We'd better go down and talk to the police."

Alexa laughed. "The 'police' is one of the habitués of the cafe. You probably saw him while you were staying there. I somehow doubt that he'll come up here with a team to dust for fingerprints and look for clues."

Mark shook his head. "I'm not surprised, but it has to be reported just the same."

"I suppose so," Alexa agreed. "But there's no reason for both of us to go." She glanced at her watch. "I'll make the report, assuming I can find old Costa, and be back within an hour."

"All right," Mark agreed, "but be careful."

"Mark—"

"I'm serious, Alexa. Someone broke into your house and stole a document. We don't know why, but there's obviously a reason, and that reason might cause danger for you. Go straight to the village and back, and keep on the road."

Alexa nodded. "I'll be back before you miss me."

That prediction didn't take into account the island ways. Unable to find Costa at his office, Alexa stopped by his home and finally discovered him at the taverna having a coffee with his cronies.

Alexa went through her story several times, observing that the crowd around the table enlarged greatly with each telling. As she'd expected, there was little Costa could do except commiserate over the vagaries and tribulations of modern life and advise everyone to watch out for suspicious characters.

That precipitated a long conversation about the various people who'd come and gone on the ferry the day before and speculation as to which of them might be the villain.

As she was leaving, Niko brought out her mail. "One from your parents," he told her, "and another from Rhodes, about the refrigerator you ordered, I expect."

Alexa thanked Niko without any rancor over his careful study of her letters. At least he didn't open and read them; she might as well be grateful for that.

Deciding to save the letter from her parents to savor later, Alexa ripped open the one from Rhodes. Niko was right, of course. Her refrigerator had arrived. That was the good side. The bad was so typical that Alexa could only shake her head. There was no one available to bring it over for another two weeks. If she wanted the refrigerator right away, she'd have to send someone for it.

Look what we've got for you:

Get 4 FREE full-length Silhouette Intimate Moments® novels.

Plus this lovely bracelet watch

Plus a surprise free gift

▼ PLUS LOTS MORE! MAIL THIS CARD TODAY ▼

Silhouette's Best-Ever "Get Acquainted" Offer

Yes, I'll try Silhouette Books under the terms outlined on the opposite page. Send me 4 free Silhouette Intimate Moments novels, a free bracelet watch and a free mystery gift.

240 CIS YADP

PLACE STICKER FOR 6 FREE GIFTS HERE

NAME _____

ADDRESS _____ APT. _____

CITY _____

STATE _____ ZIP CODE _____

PRINTED IN U.S.A.

Don't forget...

. . . Return this card today and receive 4 free books, free bracelet watch and free mystery gift.

. . . You will receive books before they're available in stores and at a discount off the cover prices.

. . . No obligation to buy. You can cancel at any time by writing ''cancel'' on your statement or returning a shipment to us at our cost.

If offer card is missing, write to: Silhouette Books
901 Fuhrmann Blvd., P.O. Box 1867, Buffalo, N.Y. 14269-1867

"I'll go over and get it," Mark told her when Alexa walked into the house dejectedly. "Don't worry."

"But Mark, that's another day wasted."

"You want the refrigerator right away, don't you?"

"Of course. I've wanted it for weeks, but I've managed without it."

"By going to the store every day, which has also wasted time. No, Alexa, it makes sense for me to make the trip. I can pick up the pipe fittings for the sink while I'm there," he reminded her.

"That's true," Alexa agreed, finally admitting, "I just don't like you being gone a whole day."

"Neither do I," Mark said. "Maybe you should come, too."

"That sounds wonderful, but we both know it's not cost effective," she said in her most businesslike manner. "I'll stay. It'll only be for twenty-four hours."

"During which I want you to be very careful. I'll get the ferry this afternoon and come back tomorrow, but you must promise not to stay here alone. Go and spend the night with your aunt."

"You're very bossy."

"Which has been your province in the past, but today it's mine. Indulge me, please." Mark touched her face with the familiar gesture that made Alexa shiver with excitement. "You know I'd rather be here," he said, "sleeping with you."

"I know," she said, "and I'll go to Sophie's."

"Good girl. Now, there's one other thing. Don't go running around in the hills by yourself and don't go down to the beach. And please, no boat rides with the Whitfields."

"The Whitfields? Do you think they had something to do with the break-in? That's impossible, Mark. They were with us." She put her hands on her hips and looked at him with a frown. "You're becoming paranoid, not to mention obsessed about the Whitfields."

"Just cautious, love," he said jokingly, in his most British accent. "But make me happy and do as I say, just for twenty-four hours."

Alexa reached up and put her arms around his neck. He felt so good, so strong. "All right." She kissed him lingeringly on the lips. "But I'll miss you."

"I'll be back. Nothing could keep me away." He held her close, and with her head nestled against his chest, Alexa couldn't see the frown on his face. "And when I get back," he said, "we'll need to have a long talk."

Alexa felt her heart pounding. "That sounds serious, Mark. About us?"

"Yep," he answered. "About us. There're some things I need to tell you."

"Now you're making me curious. What's this all about?"

"We'll talk tomorrow, Alexa. It's not the kind of thing you tell before sailing away."

It *was* serious, Alexa thought as she held onto him tightly.

"It's going to be all right, Alexa."

"Do you promise?"

"I promise."

Chapter 7

The ferry churned across choppy seas toward Rhodes City. Maybe this trip was fortuitous, Mark thought. He needed to get to a phone, a safe one where he could hear and not be heard, unlike the public phone in the *taverna*.

Mark stood at the bow of the boat alone, the spray stinging his face, and took the time to think everything out. London would have the facts he needed about the Whitfields. He could guarantee they weren't brother and sister—and that their name sure as hell wasn't Whitfield. Long years of practicing deception had taught Mark to recognize that talent in others.

Of course, Alexa saw only the good in everyone. She wouldn't understand lying in the Whitfields. Or in him. She was too accepting and trusting, and that's why he felt so bad—and so damned good.

Standing at the rail with the sea spray cooling him, Mark thought about his decision. As soon as he got back to Kavos, he was going to tell Alexa who he was and why he was there. He had no choice. In the beginning it had been just another mission, another game of wits. He hadn't expected Alexa to be what she was. She had turned everything around, and now it was much more than a job.

He hadn't counted on liking her so much. He sure as hell hadn't counted on falling in love with her. But that's just what he'd done, and now he needed to bring the game-playing to an end.

He'd tell her the truth—that he'd been sent there to find a lost artifact, the statue of Aphrodite. The statue was valuable not only because it was gold, but because it was the key to important Greek-British negotiations. He would tell her all that. Then they'd look for the statue together, and they'd find it.

He hadn't told Alexa at first for the simple reason that he'd been on assignment, with a job to do, and he hadn't known what kind of woman she was. He knew now, and he'd trust her with his life.

The wind was building. Mark pulled the collar of his jacket around his neck and stood at the rail for a while longer before heading for the bar, confident that he and Alexa could find the lost Aphrodite together. The clue was in that letter from her grandfather. He'd suspected it, and maybe the Whitfields had, too.

Alexa was working in one of the guest bedrooms, fantasizing about what she could do and then tempering her dreams with what was feasible. With a little judicious decorating, she could come up with a look that was simple and uncluttered, but at the same time comfortable and homey. Visions of the finished room danced around in her head as she poured paint into the tray, coated the roller and started on the wall.

After a while she stopped, wiped her forehead with the back of her paint-free hand and cocked her head to one side. It sounded as if someone were calling her name, but it was only her imagination, Alexa decided. No one would be around at this time of day except Sophie, who wouldn't stand on formalities. She'd come in, commenting on the progress Alexa was making as she climbed the stairs and headed down the hall.

Then Alexa heard it again and put down the roller, wary after the warnings Mark had left with her. Wiping the paint off her cheek but managing to smear it on her nose instead, Alexa went onto the balcony and peeked over, standing back in the shadows to prevent anyone from seeing her.

"Alexa," the voice called, "may I come up?"

It was Charlotte. With a sigh of relief, Alexa yelled over the edge of the roof, "No, it's a mess up here. I'll come down."

When she did, Charlotte was waiting at the bottom of the stairs. "My dear, I came as soon as I heard the news. It's all over town."

For a flash, Alexa thought Charlotte was talking about her relationship with Mark. Then she remembered the break-in.

"We've gotten everything back together," she assured her new friend. "It was just a nuisance."

"Oh, I'm sure it was more than that," Charlotte responded. "You must be terribly nervous, but of course you have Mark here as protection in case the hoodlums return.''

''Actually Mark's gone to Rhodes, but there's nothing to worry about.'' Alexa was determined that Charlotte's warnings wouldn't bring back the case of nerves she'd only just managed to get under control.

''Nothing to worry about!'' Charlotte seemed aghast. ''My dear, don't be silly. You simply can't stay here alone. Come to the boat with us while Mark's gone.''

''No, I'm fine,'' Alexa said, realizing that she meant it. ''I don't feel nervous at all during the day and to-night I'll stay at my aunt's house.''

The two women walked inside where only a few overturned objects remained as evidence of what had happened the night before.

''What did they take?'' Charlotte asked. ''Jewelry, valuables?''

''Nothing.''

''Nothing?'' Charlotte's voice was unbelieving.

''Well, nothing of monetary value. As far as I can determine, there isn't anything missing except a will and a letter from my grandfather.''

''Oh, yes, your grandfather,'' Charlotte said somewhat knowingly.

With a slight frown creasing her forehead, Alexa suggested they go into the kitchen and have coffee.

By the time she went through all the steps of Greek coffee-making, Alexa had shed her confusion and was feeling almost like herself. ''Let's sit out in the shade of the olive trees,'' she suggested, and Charlotte readily agreed.

They drank the strong, thick liquid in silence, listening to the sounds of the island—the breeze in the trees, the birds calling overhead and the drone of nearby insects.

Alexa was completely relaxed when Charlotte's words turned her around, forever, she suspected.

"My dear," Charlotte said softly, leaning toward Alexa although there was no one to hear, "I don't suppose there's any way to tell you this but straight out."

"Charlotte, what is it?" Alexa could feel her heart pounding in her chest, as if she were anticipating something awful.

"It's about Mark."

For a split second, Alexa wondered if she hadn't expected that.

"I'm glad he isn't here this morning so I can confide in you, even though this is a bad time, coming so soon after your burglary."

"Charlotte, tell me," Alexa insisted. "What about Mark?"

"Well, I'm sure this will make you very angry, but please believe that I'm telling you because I care. We both do, my brother and I."

"Charlotte, for goodness' sake, you're driving me crazy. *What* about Mark?"

"You know that Tony and I have a ship to shore radio?"

"Yes," Alexa answered impatiently.

"Well, we've made use of it, Alexa. To find out who he is."

"What do you mean?" Alexa felt herself grow cold all over, even though she'd just taken a sip of hot coffee. It turned icy in her stomach.

"Alexa, he appeared out of nowhere, didn't he?"

Alexa was angered by that. "Yes, he did. And so, I might add, did you and Tony."

"We weren't wearing knapsacks, Alexa, and we didn't move in with you. We're tourists in the islands. But Mark—"

Alexa's indignation was building. "You had no right to pry into my life, Charlotte."

"That's what I told Tony, but he insisted that you could be in trouble so I let him make some calls. I didn't think anything would turn up, Alexa. I really believed that Mark was just a well-educated drifter, and I wanted to be proved right, believe me."

Alexa almost lashed out then, almost told Charlotte to take her snooping ways and leave, go back to the boat and sail away with her brother. But something made her want to hear Charlotte out, though she didn't believe for a moment that the Whitfields could have discovered anything damaging about Mark.

Her anger controlled, Alexa said coolly, "So tell me what you and Tony found out."

"Well, all right. If you're sure." Charlotte seemed almost reluctant, but Alexa imagined that was part of the scenario. It was all a sham; she was a fool to even listen.

"His name is Mark Everett."

"I already knew that. Did it surprise you?"

"No," Charlotte said, "but the rest surprised me. He's in no way a drifter or a scholar or a dilettante or whatever he's pretended to be. But he is quite well known in England.''

''As what?'' Alexa was incredulous and yet mystified.

''As an investigative reporter. It seems he has come here to Kavos to investigate you.''

Alexa almost laughed in relief. ''Investigate me? Charlotte, that is truly absurd. You and Tony are way off base.'' Relief flooded through Alexa as she added, ''My life is an open book; there's nothing to investigate.''

''Well, if not you, then someone close to you.'' Charlotte looked away, lines of concern etched on her lovely face. ''This isn't easy for me to say.''

Alexa was truly confused. ''What in the world are you talking about?''

''Mark is on assignment, the key reporter in a huge investigation of Nazi sympathizers that is dredging up all kinds of old rumors from the past. Even the royal family isn't exempt. He's come here to Kavos to do an exposé on your grandfather and look into the possibility that he worked hand in glove with the Nazis here on Kavos.''

Alexa was totally confounded. The whole thing was preposterous, and she didn't have any intention of listening further. ''In the first place,'' she said, ''you're talking nonsense. In the second place, I wonder what kind of magical ship-to-shore arrangement you have that gives you such in-depth information about someone with nothing to go on but his name. I can't take any of this seriously, Charlotte.'' Alexa started to get up and walk away, as she knew she should have done long before.

"I don't blame you, Alexa. I would be skeptical too, but it can all be documented."

Alexa sat back down.

"The fact that he's a reporter is common knowledge," Charlotte continued. "As for the story he's working on, well, Tony is in the publishing business, and his contacts are beyond reproach. It's true, Alexa."

But as soon as she made that statement, Charlotte attempted to take it back. "I only mean it's true that he's working on a collaboration story. We don't believe for a moment that your grandfather was involved. That's just speculation."

"And the rest is fact?" Alexa was feeling suddenly numb.

"Yes."

"Pappous couldn't have been a collaborator," Alexa said fiercely, trying not to think about the whispered conversations she had heard so long ago, the way that even Vassili and Sophie refused to talk about the war.

"It couldn't be true," Alexa said at last, sinking back against the tree, her face white.

"Not about your grandfather, Alexa. I just can't believe that. But it's true that Mark hopes to prove it. That's why he's here."

"What could he possibly accomplish by that?" Alexa asked, trying not to think about how Mark had insinuated himself into her life and gotten close to her. So very close. Alexa felt a sob building inside, and Charlotte covered Alexa's hand with her own.

She didn't realize, Alexa thought, just how terrible this really was because Charlotte didn't know what Mark meant to her.

"He's looking for a bestseller, I imagine," Charlotte answered. "Or a made-for-television movie. Money, my dear."

Alexa felt a low moan escape her lips, but Charlotte didn't seem to notice as she continued. "You should hear about the schemes he's used to get information about people." Charlotte lowered her eyes, and Alexa suddenly knew the other woman was thinking.

"No," Alexa denied dully.

"He came out of nowhere," Charlotte reminded her. "Just when you needed him. He helped you out, even though he's not really a carpenter. That must be obvious," Charlotte suggested.

"Yes, it is," Alexa admitted. He'd been willing, and that had made up for his limited skills. Now she realized that he had had an ulterior motive, a terrible one.

"It wasn't coincidence," Charlotte said finally.

"No, it wasn't." Somehow Alexa had known all along that Mark's appearance was more a result of calculation rather than of chance, but she hadn't been able to face it. Charlotte had torn away the veil of her denial and made her look at herself and Mark. He'd used her in so many ways. She hated him; she hated herself.

Charlotte's arm went around her shoulder, and Alexa felt comfort in it. She rested her cheek against Charlotte's hand and breathed a deep sigh.

"This has devastated you," Charlotte said. "I knew you'd be upset, but I didn't expect your reaction to be this intense. Please, come back to the boat with me. Maybe talking with Tony will help. He's concerned about you.''

The last thing Alexa wanted at this point was Tony hovering over her. ''No,'' she said with what politeness she could muster. ''I need to be alone for a while.''

''I understand that,'' Charlotte said, ''but I feel terrible leaving you. Are you sure you'll be all right?''

Alexa got to her feet and forced a smile. ''I'll be fine. It's just that I have so much to digest. Mark—a reporter who came here on assignment. My grandfather—a Nazi collaborator.''

''I'm sorry, my dear. So sorry.''

''It's not your fault, Charlotte. I'm not going to imitate the Greeks of old and kill the bearer of bad tidings.''

They both managed a faint laugh at that.

''When I've dealt with this,'' Alexa said, ''then we can talk. Please thank Tony for caring.''

Charlotte got up, brushed the twigs and grass from her skirt and walked with Alexa to the house. At the gate she paused and said, ''I worry about you being alone. If you absolutely refuse to come to us, maybe we should stay here.''

''No,'' Alexa said. ''I'll be fine, and if there's any problem, I'll go to my aunt's house. Don't worry.''

''All right,'' Charlotte answered, kissing Alexa on the cheek. ''Do try to get some sleep, as difficult as that may seem. It really would help.''

''I know,'' Alexa said, confident that she wouldn't close her eyes that night.

Charlotte turned once more to wave before she went out through the heavy oak gate and started down the mountain.

Alexa had forgotten about her before Charlotte reached the first curve in the road. But she hadn't forgotten the news Charlotte had brought to Villa Alexi. She'd never forget that. It would change everything; it would change her life.

For a long tortuous time after Charlotte left, Alexa thought about Mark. She tried not to, but it was no use; everything came rushing back.

Alexa remembered the first time she'd seen him, smiling boyishly, full of ideas for remodeling her house. And his ideas had worked, most of them. Even if he hadn't been a carpenter, he'd gotten things done. *They'd* gotten things done. Together. She remembered the rest, too. Their nights of lovemaking that had seemed so very right. Alexa shivered involuntarily. Just like with everything else in her life, she'd made a wrong choice.

Even coming back to Kavos had been wrong for the woman who was her grandfather's favorite, the granddaughter of a collaborator. That's what he was, Alexa admitted to herself. It all fit together perfectly.

In one fell swoop she'd lost the two men who'd meant the most to her. Alexa had always felt closer to Pappous than to her father. And she'd never loved anyone the way she had, briefly, loved Mark.

She wished that he were here now so that she could confront him. She wanted to be face-to-face with Mark, shout her accusations and hear his response. She imagined he would be quick enough to find some explanation, but whatever it was, it wouldn't be good enough to satisfy her. Not after the way she'd been used.

Then, as she was heading back into the house, Alexa remembered something. Before Mark had left he'd told her that they needed to talk. This must be the subject of their discussion. His confession.

Alexa stopped with her hand on the front-door knob. If Mark was a journalist, he wasn't a very good one. She was fairly certain that he'd found out nothing about Pappous. Well, she would find out herself, once and for all. She turned away from the house, walked back to the gate and headed with determination down the hill to Sophie's.

Her aunt was in the kitchen cooking, her hands deep in a bowl of flour. "Come on in," she called out. "I'm making *kourabiedes*."

"My favorite," Alexa said automatically.

"Your grandfather's, too. Your great-grandmother used to make them for us when we were children. We'd hang around the kitchen table, watching her, poking our fingers into the dough for a taste when she wasn't looking."

Sophie reached for the whiskey bottle and measured two ounces into the flour mixture. "They're wedding cookies, you know," she said to Alexa.

"I know," Alexa responded. Her words were still coming automatically; she wasn't thinking about the cookies at all.

"You like them nice and big, don't you, palm-size, not those tiny anemic ones they sell at the bakery shop?" Sophie asked her niece as she pulled off a big hunk of the mixture, which she flattened before placing it on the baking sheet.

"Yes," Alexa answered.

She continued to watch until Sophie put the cookies into the oven, wiped her hands on her apron, heaved a sigh and lowered herself into a chair opposite Alexa.

"Now tell me what's the matter, child. You look terrible," Sophie said bluntly.

"It's—" Alexa couldn't find the words. "I want to talk about Pappous," she said finally.

"Of course," Sophie responded. "Don't we talk about him all the time?"

"This is different. I've heard...someone said... Oh, Aunt Sophie, he's been accused of working for the Nazis during the war."

"This is true, Alexa," Sophie said calmly. Alexa's hands flew to her mouth, and before she could utter a sound Sophie continued, "He used to take them from island to island in his boat. He helped unload and catalog their supplies." Sophie shook her head thoughtfully. "Those were terrible days, during the war. A man had to protect himself and his family."

"But to collaborate with the Nazis!" Alexa's words were wrenched from her.

"Oh, no, my dear," Sophie said. "He was not one of those."

"I thought you said—"

"Of course, he did their work, but whenever he could, he learned their secrets. He passed information on to the British. There was a soldier here, a sergeant, I believe, who was Alexi's contract—is that the word?"

"Contact," Alexa said with a sigh of relief.

"Yes, contact. They worked together, the sergeant and Alexi. They tried to make life difficult for the Nazis. Many times your grandfather's life was in danger, but he kept on with his work."

"He was a hero!" Alexa said with a gasp. "Then why didn't everyone know about it? Why all the secrecy?"

Sophie looked across at her great-niece with a serious expression. "It is not our way to talk of these things," she explained. "Many men were killed, both Greek and Nazi. Your grandfather himself killed. So did Vassili and Niko's father and Yianni's. We do not talk about it. The men did what they had to do, but they have all asked forgiveness of the priest and of God and put it behind them. So be it," she finished.

Alexa's head was reeling. Her grandfather was a hero. He might have done terrible things, but it had been in wartime, and he was still a hero, not a collaborator, not a traitor.

"Now that I have told you," Sophie was saying, "I want you to forget all about it. That is what Alexi would want." She leaned over and opened the oven door. "The cookies will be done soon. Will you wait?"

Alexa got up and hugged Sophie. "Not this time, but I'll be back. In fact, I'm coming to spend the night if that's all right."

"You know it is," Sophie said.

"Now I want to go home for a little while. I need some time to think."

Alexa's head was still reeling when she reached the house. Her grandfather wasn't a collaborator, and

Mark had no story! But there was more. If it wasn't true about Alexi, then maybe it wasn't true about Mark, either. Maybe Charlotte was a liar. Alexa had to find out. Slowly she climbed the stairs to the room where Mark had stored his belongings, anxious to know and yet afraid.

Unsure of where to begin, Alexa opened a bureau drawer and emptied it onto the bed. She'd never searched anyone's room before, and she felt like a criminal at worst, snoop at best, looking through his personal belongings. But why not? This was certainly no worse than Mark passing himself off as someone else, no matter what the motive.

There was nothing in his knapsack but books, most of them in Greek, a few in English. There wasn't even a passport. He'd taken that to Rhodes. There were no notebooks or even any notes. Whatever his scholarly goals, Mark hadn't pursued them during this time on Kavos.

Alexa opened the books and began looking through them carefully, one at a time. Inside a volume of Sophocles' plays, she finally found a piece of paper covered with writing in modern Greek. She paused and tried to read it, although she never had been able to read Greek very well. Then she saw her own name and realized that she was holding in her hand a copy of the letter her grandfather had written to her, the letter that was attached to his will, the letter that had been stolen.

She dropped into a chair, staring stupidly at the page. Over every word or two Mark had made a penciled notation, as if he'd been trying to decipher something, as if he thought the letter was in code!

Alexa tried to reason things out as best she could, asking herself pertinent questions. Had Mark copied the letter before or after it had been stolen, what was his reason for copying it and why hadn't he told her?

There were no logical answers. She suddenly knew less about Mark than she'd known when they first met. Only one thing was clear to her—she could never trust him again.

When Mark returned the next afternoon, Alexa was at the kitchen table. It was twilight, and she was sitting in the semidarkness without having lit any of the lamps.

"I'm finally back," he said as he burst through the door, gave her a quick kiss on the cheek and explained, "The ferry was late, of course. Your refrigerator is down at the docks, but I'll have to hire a donkey to get it up here." He emptied his knapsack on the table. "I had a terrible time finding—"

He stopped long enough to take everything in—the faint light, her silence and, when he reached for the switch and illuminated the room, the book on the table in front of her.

"You found it," he said simply.

"I found it," she answered.

"Then it's past time for our talk." He reached for her hand, still and white on the table. "I'm so sorry, Alexa, but I can explain."

She pulled her hand back as if she'd been burned. "It's well past time, Mark. It may even be too late."

"No," he said quickly. "It's not too late. Just tell me what you want to know, where you want me to begin."

"At the beginning, I suppose," she answered dully. "With your name. Is it Mark Everett?"

"That's a name I use sometimes. My real name is Mark Graham. I have a passport and ID in the name of Mark Everett."

"Are you a reporter?"

"What?" He seemed genuinely surprised. "No. Where did you get that idea?"

Alexa's voice was suspicious. "Charlotte said—"

"Oh, so that's it," Mark interrupted. "I wouldn't believe much of what the Whitfields tell you."

"But I should believe *you*?"

"Yes," he said. "From this moment. I'll tell you the plain facts. I work for the British government."

Alexa's eyes narrowed.

"For Intelligence," he continued. "I'm . . . I guess you could say I'm a secret agent."

Alexa responded with a laugh. "What kind of fool do you take me for, Mark?" she asked. "Do you really think I'm going to believe that you're an agent on some kind of mission?" Her voice was dry, her tone sarcastic.

Mark tried to answer in a way that would make her understand. "I suppose I'm on a mission of sorts, but it's not official. My godfather, Sir William Brevort of the British Museum, asked me to come over and locate an artifact for him."

Alexa let out a deep sigh. It was obvious to Mark that she wasn't going to give him a chance to explain. "Mr. Graham," she said in her coldest tone, "you are beneath contempt. If you're going to lie at least make it plausible. When the Whitfields said you were a reporter digging up facts about the Nazi occupation, that was more believable than this! I don't want to hear any more.''

Alexa stood up and started to leave the room, but before she reached the door Mark was after her. He grabbed her arm and spun her around. "You wanted the truth, Alexa, and that's what I'm giving you. At least have the decency to hear me out."

She tried to pull away, but he wouldn't let her. His grip on her arm was unrelenting. "Hear me out," he repeated angrily. "Then if you want me to leave, fine. But dammit, listen to me first."

Alexa let herself be pulled back to the table where she sank onto the chair like a rag doll.

"You've heard me talk about my godfather, how he brought me to Greece and taught me to love the country. He always wanted me to be an archeologist, but I chose another profession."

"Government agent?" she asked disbelievingly.

"Yes," he answered, "though that's another story. I won't bore you with it now, but believe me, it's true. When my godfather needed some special work done here, he asked me, and I agreed, unofficially."

"But secretly," she said without hiding her bitterness.

"I was wrong not to tell you, Alexa," he admitted. "But I didn't know anything about you or how you'd react. Then when I decided to come clean—well, the trip to Rhodes interfered. And quite honestly," he met her eyes directly, trying not to flinch at the anger he saw, "after years of deceit on the job, it was easier to lie than to tell the truth."

"That I believe," she said, watching him with narrowed eyes.

Mark didn't miss the look. It hurt him deeply, and he only hoped that he could change it and get everything back to the way it had been before.

He continued his explanation. "Sir William was asked by the prime minister to return an artifact to Greece. It was a gate of Aphrodite that had been removed from the country during the war. In an effort to promote goodwill between the two countries, the government decided to make a gesture by returning the gate. A date was set for the ceremony, June 12." He looked at his watch. "Five days from now."

Alexa was silent.

Mark almost shrugged. It seemed hopeless, but all he could do was tell the truth. "Sir William sent his assistant down to the vaults of the museum where the Aphrodite gate was supposedly stored...."

He let the sentence dangle, but Alexa was having none of it. "I don't want to play guessing games, Mark," she said through clenched teeth. "Just tell your story."

"Part of the gate was there, the statues of Athena and Hera that flanked Aphrodite. But the goddess of love was gone."

"Stolen?" Alexa couldn't prevent herself from asking.

"Not stolen, at least not from the museum. It seems that Aphrodite was lifted while the statue was still in Greece during World War II." He scrutinized her face, but it remained unresponsive, closed.

Mark went on. "The Nazis had removed it from a site in the Peloponnisos and transported it here to Kavos. That's when it vanished."

"You're saying someone on Kavos is involved." It wasn't a question.

Mark answered anyway. "Yes, I am. A British sergeant and a Greek resistance fighter took the gate from the Nazis. The sergeant was determined to take it to England and give it to the British Museum, but the Greek didn't like that idea, so he 'liberated' the central piece of the group, the Aphrodite. Hera and Athena went on to England, but Aphrodite was never found. The sergeant is certain it's still here on Kavos, where it was hidden by the resistance fighter."

"Who is supposedly my grandfather," Alexa said, responding at last, though with the same air of denial.

"Doesn't it add up, Alexa? Just think."

"You only have some sergeant's word." She continued to fight what was becoming obvious.

"His sworn testimony. Why would he lie?"

"That's simple, Mark. He would lie if he stole the statue himself."

"It never left the island," Mark answered matter-of-factly. "Alexi hid the statue, and now we need it. Badly. This is very involved, Alexa, and it may not sound serious, but believe me, it is. For the sake of Greek-British relations, we need the statue. The date is set."

"You mean your government is actually going through with the ceremony with only part of this . . . this gate?"

"We have no choice. Wheels were put into motion long before we discovered the gate wasn't complete. Now if we announce we've 'misplaced' the most important part of the gate, which, for all intents purposes, we stole in the first place, the anti-British press in Greece will have a field day.''

Alexa almost laughed. If that happened, she wouldn't feel so bad.

''I know, on a personal level, it's almost amusing, but think of the political and economic repercussions, Alexa. There's guilt associated with the theft, some bad feelings connected with the return, and a great deal of embarrassment over the fact that someone outsmarted them all.''

''Pappous,'' she said.

''Yes, Pappous. If the Aphrodite turns up hidden here on Kavos, all of the meaning of England's gesture will be defeated, Alexa. It's pure and simple politics. And it's important, believe me. The shape of the world these days hardly allows for even the smallest embarrassments between allied nations.''

Alexa could understand that. But Mark's connection to the situation was another matter. ''So you were supposed to zoom over here, get friendly with me and find Aphrodite?''

Mark felt ashamed under her cold-eyed scrutiny, but he tried to be honest. ''Basically, that's it.''

''You didn't feel it necessary to tell me or let me in on your little secret.'' Again, it was a statement, not a question.

''I was going to tell you tonight.''

''Oh, yes, now that your seduction of me is complete. I guess that makes everything different and special.'' Her voice vibrated with hurt and bitterness.

He knew Alexa was still angry, and he couldn't blame her. As much as he wanted to reach out to her,

Mark restrained himself, knowing she would only push him away.

"I didn't seduce you," he said evenly. "I wanted you and you wanted me, and don't try to deny that." Mark could feel his own anger rising now. In her pain, she was twisting everything.

"I guess we were both wrong." Alexa got up again, and handed him the book. "By the way, Mark," she asked, almost in passing, "why did you copy the letter?"

"It seemed like a clue of sorts. Your grandfather mentioned a secret, and I thought there might be a code in it to the whereabouts of the statue."

"My, you are clever, Mr. Agent. I'm tremendously impressed." Alexa gestured around the house. "Please feel free to have a look, not that you haven't already during all those night raids on the kitchen." She smiled sweetly. "Did you pay to have the house burgled, too?"

"Of course not, Alexa. That's a hell of a thing to say."

"Oh, I'm so sorry to offend." She turned and started out the door.

"Where are you going?"

"Out. And I may not be back until tomorrow when I expect you to be gone."

Chapter 8

Alexa stumbled down the hill in the darkness, cursing because she hadn't brought a flashlight, but well aware that when she'd been confronted with Mark's feeble explanation she'd had no thought except to escape, to get away from him and from his lies. A flashlight had hardly figured in that plan.

Besides, she hadn't known where she was going, and yet somehow the obvious place hadn't seemed right to her, so Alexa had kept running, past Sophie's house. Now she was on the road that wound upward even further into the hills.

She'd long since stopped running and was going at a pace that was difficult in the rocky terrain but that seemed necessary if she were to outrun the demons that were still threatening her.

And Alexa had every intention of doing just that.

She could see nothing but somehow knew that she was on friendly ground. Even in the black night, there was a feeling of security. It was because she'd come to Vassili's house. Somehow she'd known that was where she'd been headed. She didn't need Sophie now—she needed a man, a man who'd been with her grandfather during the war, who probably knew what had really happened.

Sophie had told Alexa everything she knew; now it was time to talk to Vassili. During her flight to him, Alexa had realized that even Vassili might not be aware of the truth, but there was no one else on Kavos she could even approach. He was her only hope.

At first Vassili hadn't even been willing to listen, not that he'd been unsympathetic, far from it. He'd poured her a cup of coffee, added a splash of brandy and sat back, arms folded, at the table.

But he wasn't letting himself get involved in her plight. He might as well have been in another world for all the acknowledgement he gave her. Unlike Sophie, he didn't plead ignorance or fear. He simply patted her hand and remained silent.

Then Alexa got angry. She confronted him with the facts as she knew them, laying out all the specifics for Vassili and daring him to deny anything. She spoke in Greek to eliminate the excuse that he didn't understand, and when the spiel was over Alexa knew she had him.

"Vassili?" she asked, "what is the answer?"

He took a long swig of the coffee he'd generously laced with brandy and heaved a weighty Greek sigh.

"It is true," he said of her story. "A colonel in the SS came to Kavos from the Peloponnisos with the gate that you speak of. They killed him."

"They?" Alexa asked, knowing the answer, but ready now for all the specifics.

"Alexi and the British sergeant." After another swig, Vassili continued. "The sergeant was determined to take the treasure home with him as a prize of war, and Alexi let him believe that that was possible. In a way it was, but the sergeant didn't allow for your grandfather's persistence. The Englishman got away with the gate and never knew until recently that the most important figure, the golden Aphrodite, was missing."

"Golden?" Alexa asked.

"Oh, yes," Vassili told her. "The other figures were bronze, but the goddess of love was made of solid gold."

Alexa barely restrained herself from gasping.

"The poor soldier, ignorant of your grandfather's ruse, returned to England, and I suppose Alexi had the last laugh."

"Where did he hide it?" Alexa asked, trying her best to sound casual.

But her tone of voice wouldn't have mattered. Neither Vassili nor anyone else knew the whereabouts of the statue.

"He never told us," Vassili said.

And so Alexi, worried that the British might some day come for the treasure, had taken his secret to the grave. That had been his own private joke.

* * *

After leaving Vassili's, Alexa stood at the crest of the hill watching the lights flickering in the windows of her house and facing the fact that everything Mark had told her was true. But there was one thing he hadn't mentioned—that the Aphrodite was made of gold.

When she got to the bottom of the hill, Alexa pushed open the gate, crossed the courtyard and went into the kitchen.

Mark was standing at the stove cooking as if nothing had happened. Somehow she hadn't expected that. Without turning around he said, "I'm making scrambled eggs and toast. There's enough for you. Want to join me?"

"No," she said and then quickly changed her mind. "I mean yes." She was starving.

"Then have a seat," Mark said, gesturing with the spatula. "There's a pot of tea on the stove. Want a cup?"

Alexa almost laughed aloud at that. "There'll always be an England," she said, pouring them both tea. She put sugar in her cup and handed the other one, filled with the strong, almost black brew, to Mark before returning to the table.

Mark's response was a silent smile as he served the eggs and toast. For a while they ate in silence.

"Where have you been?" he asked finally.

"To Vassili's," she responded.

"Did he confirm what I told you?"

"Essentially, yes," Alexa said, "except he also mentioned that the Aphrodite was made of gold. I didn't know that." Her voice was accusatory.

"I would have told you," he answered somewhat defensively.

"I guess that makes the stakes a lot higher," she said.

He shook his head. "The Greek government would want it back whether it was gold, bronze or tin, but let's say it makes the loss more dramatic. Aphrodite is worth an enormous amount of money, something the Whitfields certainly realize."

Alexa had no answer for that understatement. "What are you going to do now?" she asked finally.

"I'm going to hope that the owner of Villa Alexi will let me stay and search for the statue. I still have some time left."

"You really believe you can find it?"

"I've had experience in this kind of thing, Alexa," he said, "and I don't intend to fail this time for Sir William's sake. He's a very fine old man, and he feels personally responsible for this foul-up. I'd hate to see him with egg on his face."

"Do you think Pappous's letter is really in code?" she asked.

Mark shook his head. "I'm sure it's not. Unfortunately," he added. "That would have made it easy."

"You must be some sort of expert at breaking codes," she said.

Mark smiled. "Actually, I am." The answer wasn't a boast, just a statement of fact.

Alexa accepted it as such, no longer inclined to question him.

When they finished eating and had cleared the table, she opened a cabinet door and told him, "Aunt Sophie made some cookies. Would you like one?"

"More than one," Mark admitted.

Alexa brought over the whole platter of the Greek cookies and they both dug in.

"They're *kourabiedes*," he said. "My favorites."

"Mine, too," Alexa told him.

He smiled at her. His expression was familiar, even intimate, but it didn't get an answering smile in return. She was still staying a little removed from Mark after what had happened between them, and she intended to keep her distance.

"I'd like for you to help me find the statue," he said. "I know that I should have asked you that first day, and I realize that I've messed things up pretty badly."

Alexa nodded. She wasn't about to let him off the hook.

"However," Mark went on, "I've apologized. I'm not going any further than that."

"I didn't think you would," she answered.

"But you'd like me to."

"I'm still angry, Mark. Naturally I'd like you to be contrite, but I certainly don't expect it."

"But you will help me find the Aphrodite?"

"Of course. I'd like to have everything resolved, too. After all, I suppose you could say my grandfather stole the statue, and it should go back to wherever it belongs."

"At the temple of Aphrodite near Memnope in the Peloponnisos."

"Do you have any idea where my grandfather hid the statue?"

"Not a one. I've looked all over the house. It's not here."

"He could have hidden it anywhere," Alexa mused aloud. "On the beach, in the hills."

"But he probably didn't," Mark told her. "He would have wanted the statue nearby where it would be safe and he could watch over it."

"The garden," Alexa said.

"I've thought about that, but it's enormous, and since there isn't a bulldozer handy on Kavos to dig it all up, where do we begin?"

Alexa shrugged. "There's still a possibility it's in the house," she told him.

"As I said, Alexa—"

"I know. You're good at this sort of thing, but I'm a woman with intuition, which I plan to use. Let's start on the house tonight, and tomorrow we can get to the yard."

Mark smiled at her enthusiasm, reaching toward her in the old way to touch her cheek.

But things had changed. The old way didn't work anymore. Alexa drew back, and Mark dropped his hand, forcing himself to stay on the subject.

"I appreciate your help, Alexa. So will Sir William and ultimately so will the people of Greece. If we can pull this off and return the gate—"

"It would be wonderful," she said, "and I do want to help. Just remember one thing, Mark."

He looked at her warily. "What's that?"

"I still think you're a bastard."

They spent the next few hours retracing steps Mark had already taken.

"You looked inside this wall?" Alexa asked unbelievingly.

Mark nodded.

"How, when?"

"When I was working. I had to get behind there to reinforce the beams. While I was there, I looked around."

"On my time," Alexa said curtly.

Mark didn't answer. He'd admitted his mistake once, and as he'd told Alexa, he wasn't going to be contrite. But tonight the search could be more thorough with them working together, exploring all the hidden places where the statue could have been secluded. Although he hoped he was wrong, Mark didn't expect to turn up even a clue, and by the time the evening was over, they both had to admit defeat.

Exhausted and disheartened, they sat in the living room on the floor, leaning against the sofa, a bottle of Metaxa between them.

Alexa took a long sip from the glass that Mark had filled for her, choked a bit over the strong taste but tried another sip anyway to relieve the tension in the back of her neck. The brandy didn't help, and she rubbed at the painful cramp.

"Like a massage?" Mark asked.

"No, I'm fine," Alexa answered quickly if inaccurately as she inched away from him.

"Just asking." He reached for the bottle and poured himself another long drink, which he tossed down expertly, feeling only the hint of a burn. Although he rarely drank these days, there'd been a time when he'd put away much stronger stuff than this and in larger quantities. Tough remedies for a tough job. But that had been years ago.

Mark took a deep breath, stretched and rearranged his long legs. His shoulder was inches from Alexa's, his hand was close to her thigh. Forty-eight hours before he would have reached for that inviting body, and she would have responded. Now he didn't dare.

Alexa had noticed the slight movement of his hand, but hadn't needed to move away again because he'd ignored his impulse to touch her. He understood her feelings just as he seemed to understand everything about her.

She wondered if he knew what was going through her head now and sincerely hoped not. She looked over at him and almost lost her heart. His blond hair was tousled, and there was an exhausted look in his usually bright blue eyes. They seemed a shade more green, not as clear but even more entrancing. His long lashes were almost black, unexpected with his light coloring, and his strong profile was wonderfully familiar to her. She could have drawn each chiseled plane from memory, and yet she didn't know who he was, what he was.

"How did you get to be a secret agent, anyway?" she asked suddenly.

Taken aback, Mark didn't answer for a moment.

"Did you study in school," she persisted, "or was spying just a natural talent?"

Mark tried not to notice her sarcasm. "That's easy," he said. "I got to be an agent by answering an advert in the London *Times*."

"Really? I'm intrigued," she admitted.

"Intrigued with how a nice guy like me got mixed up in such a dirty business?"

"Who said you were nice?" came the rejoinder.

Mark ignored her, put his hands behind his head and said thoughtfully, "Some of what I told you was true, most of it, in fact. I did study classics at university. I was good at languages, not just French and German but the more esoteric ones, as well. Sanskrit, Assyrian and Hittite, languages that no one has spoken in centuries. To me they were like a game, a code to be broken.''

Alexa was listening with interest, and that encouraged Mark to go on. ''My parents were appalled at my choice of studies. They wanted me to be in business, banking or law. Instead they had a dilettante as a son.''

Alexa didn't say anything, but she couldn't help feeling a kinship for the man who hadn't been able to satisfy his parents' hopes. She'd had the same struggle and experienced the same feeling of defeat.

''I drifted from one translating job to another,'' Mark continued, ''without much ambition. I broke up with my girlfriend and tried my hand at teaching, which I found unbearably boring. Then I answered an advert as a lark, and the agency recruited me. I was ripe and they knew it.''

''Did you find what you were looking for there?''

Mark shook his head. ''At first I was committed to the service and the country, but little by little the glow wore off. I began to see what it was really like—a rather dirty little job, filled with petty people, lying and deception.'' He looked intently at her. ''They don't even tell the truth to someone they love,'' he said. ''It's hell on relationships. And you know what came of it all?'' He answered his own question. ''I'm still drifting.''

Alexa's gaze was riveted on his eyes, which had a green sadness in them now. It was very quiet in the room, and they sat still, side by side, not touching.

Finally Alexa spoke. "I guess we're not that different after all," she said slowly. "Two drifters who somehow ended up on Kavos."

Mark stood up and held out his hand. "Maybe we can make something good out of all this. Maybe we can find the Aphrodite."

Alexa took his hand and let him pull her to her feet. "We can give it one hell of a try," she said. "Starting with the garden tomorrow."

He let go of her hand. "Then I'll see you in the morning?" He'd meant to make that a definitive statement, but it turned into a question, and by the look in his eyes, Mark was afraid, was begging for an encouraging answer.

She didn't comply. In fact, she didn't answer at all but turned and disappeared with a quick smile down the hall into her room.

Mark reached to turn off the light and then paused, bent over, picked up the bottle of Metaxa and took it to his room.

The sun beat down on Mark as he struggled to get a foothold for his shovel under the large rock. He knew it was fruitless now, this indiscriminate digging when they had no real plan. He wasn't used to going at a project blindly, but over breakfast when he'd tried to explore the past with Alexa, she hadn't been able to remember anything pertinent. All she had was the letter and the mention of a "secret."

"I always thought he meant the secret of happiness," she told Mark, but he knew better. There *was* an answer, hidden away by an old man who wanted his granddaughter to find it but had been reluctant to tell her outright. Unfortunately, Mark believed, he'd planted the clues very carefully, where only Alexa could find them—in her mind and in her memory.

Alexa was on the other side of the garden out of sight, digging in a particularly neglected area, her theory being that Alexi had wanted it to appear neglected to hide what was underneath. But she'd found nothing, and she, too, was becoming discouraged.

The fact that Alexa was getting nothing from Mark except questions that she couldn't answer added to her discouragement. And it didn't help that everything was still strained between them. Alexa knew that was her fault, but she couldn't change her feelings, especially when he divulged what he'd learned on Rhodes about the Whitfields.

It had been shocking, and she hadn't wanted to believe it. But everything else Mark had told her fit into place, and she feared this would, too. She'd argued with him at first and then agreed to go along with his plan.

But none of what he'd told her had made their relationship any easier.

Mark realized that and it bothered him. For the moment, there was nothing he could do about it, but one thing was certain—this aimless digging would get them nowhere.

He put down the shovel and started to call to Alexa when he heard voices in the courtyard. That didn't surprise Mark. He'd been expecting a visit, and by the time the callers reached the house, he was there waiting for them.

"Everett!" Tony exclaimed in a voice that was obviously surprised. Charlotte said nothing.

"Good morning," Mark responded casually. "What can I do for you?"

"We just stopped by to see Alexa," Tony said, "and find out how she's doing."

Charlotte remained silent.

"Not very well," Mark said. "As a matter of fact, she seems to have come down with something." He was leaning against the door, a pose that was relaxed but meaningful. Obviously he had no intention of moving aside to let them in.

Tony frowned. "Really?"

Mark looked him dead in the eye. "Really," he repeated. "She had a fever when I got back so I fetched her aunt, who spent the night. She's still here, in fact, and so is her cousin. It seems the family has rallied round to nurse her."

"Oh, dear, this is dreadful," Charlotte said, her hands fluttering anxiously. "Can we do anything? May I see her?"

Mark answered her questions in order. "I don't think there's anything you can do except send your good wishes. As for seeing her, *I* haven't even done that today. The relatives have prescribed quiet, and I'm not about to challenge that. If you'd like to go up against either of them..." Mark stepped aside, leaving the doorway open.

Charlotte laughed nervously. "No, no," she said. "We'd only be in the way."

"But we will be back tomorrow," Tony added. "Please tell Alexa that and send our love."

"I will," Mark assured him.

Tony turned, taking Charlotte's arm, and started across the courtyard. Then he stopped, as if remembering something. "You know, Everett, if she needs medical care, we can take her over to Rhodes on our boat."

"Good thought," Mark said. "I'll tell her. That is, I'll tell the relatives. They're running the show."

"Yes, yes, of course," Tony said.

"Don't forget to give her our love," Charlotte admonished as the two disappeared through the gate and down the path toward town.

As soon as they were out of sight, Mark went back to the garden, calling out to Alexa, "It's all right. They've gone."

"Did they buy the story?"

Mark shrugged. "I doubt it, but at least they're confused, and with the threat of a house full of relatives, they're unlikely to try another midnight raid."

"You're sure they instigated the break-in?"

"I'm sure, Alexa."

"I just can't believe it," Alexa said, thinking about Charlotte and the couple of good times they'd shared. It was true that they hadn't known each other very long, but then Alexa hadn't known Mark long, either.

"From what my London contacts tell me," Mark continued, "they know about the Aphrodite, and they want her. You can forget any idealistic thoughts of them returning the statue to Greece," he added. "A woman fitting Charlotte's description worked for my godfather at the British Museum. She recently left the job, and her flat is empty.''

''Do you think they're—dangerous?'' It sounded so ridiculous, just saying the word.

Mark answered with a question of his own. ''Can you imagine how much this statue would be worth on the open market?'' He didn't wait for her answer. It was obvious. ''I don't know much about the Whitfields except that isn't their name. We'll wait until my contacts run their checks and let us know. Until then, we need to be careful and keep them at a distance.''

Even in the warm sun, Alexa shivered at his words.

''I'm almost too exhausted to eat,'' Alexa groaned, ''much less cook.'' They hadn't even attempted to set the table in the dining room but had stretched out on the living room sofa, their plates on their laps.

''Fortunately we were saved by your aunt and her huge tureen of soup.''

Alexa sipped a spoonful. ''And her promise to go along with the story of my illness in case the Whitfields ask.''

''I only wish she knew something about Aphrodite.''

''But she doesn't,'' Alexa said with a sigh, ''and I'm too tired to do anything now but sleep.''

''No digging by lantern light?'' he asked.

''Nope. Because it's ridiculous. You're right, Mark. We have no plan, and this blind searching is hopeless.''

Mark didn't bother to agree; it was an indisputable fact.

"Oh, Aphrodite, where are you?" Alexa asked sleepily. "*Who* are you?" She stretched back on the sofa. "Tell me about her, Mark."

"Didn't your grandfather ever tell you the stories of Aphrodite?"

"I suppose he must have, but I can't remember very much. I know that she was the goddess of love, of course."

"Married to Hephaestos, who was not only lame but also ugly. Some legends call her the daughter of Zeus; others say she sprang from the sea's foam."

"Like Botticelli's Venus?"

"Yes," he said. "She inadvertently began the Trojan war by promising Paris the most beautiful woman in the world. He chose Helen. The story is on the gate," Mark added, "the contest between Hera, Athena and Aphrodite for the golden apple."

Alexa's eyes were closed, but Mark knew she wasn't sleeping. Still, he lowered his voice. "Aphrodite stole away the wits even of the wise. The swan was sacred to her," he went on, "as well as the dove, the rose and the myrtle."

"I remember something about that," Alexa said, half awake and half asleep. "Pappous told me..." Her words faded, and her breathing became deep and regular.

Mark got up and covered her with a blanket.

When Alexa awoke, she was stiff and cramped from sleeping on the sofa. She opened her eyes, blinking in the light, which was still shining brightly from the overhead lamp. Looking across the room, she saw that Mark was asleep in the chair.

Alexa didn't know what time it was nor did she care. Something had come to her, either awake or asleep. It didn't matter. All that counted was that she had remembered. She got up and went to Mark.

"Wake up," she said, shaking him lightly.

He moaned but didn't move.

"Mark, wake up," she repeated. "I know where Aphrodite is."

That did it. Mark sat up in the chair, glancing at his watch. It was three in the morning. "Did you remember something your grandfather said?"

"Yes. No. I'm not sure."

"Alexa," Mark said, a little irritated. "It's three in the morning and you're 'not sure.'"

"I mean I'm not sure whether I remembered or whether I dreamed it, but just before I went to sleep you mentioned the sacred symbols of Aphrodite."

"Yes, the swan—"

"The dove and the myrtle," Alexa finished. "I'm sure now that Pappous told me about them when I was a child."

"That's fine, Alexa," Mark said as he patted her hand. "But it's really not a reason to wake me up."

"Unless I tell you that my grandfather buried the statue of Aphrodite beneath the myrtle and doves." Alexa was so excited that her words were falling all over one another.

"What are you talking about?"

"Remember when I mentioned the fountain at the back of the garden? Well, there are birds carved at the base of it. I thought they were pigeons, but now I'm sure they're doves."

Mark's face was expressionless as he waited.

"That statue's under the myrtle tree, Mark," she said.

"Let's get the shovels," Mark exclaimed, causing a smile to break out on Alexa's face as she jumped up and headed for the garden. "I'll bring the lantern," he called after her, but Alexa had already disappeared out the door.

Two hours later, a hazy dawn was just beginning to color the sky as Alexa opened the living room curtains. With a smile, she turned toward Mark. "We did it," she said.

"You did it," Mark corrected. "If you hadn't come up with the right place to dig, we could have spent another week in that garden. By then it would have been too late."

"Is there still time now?"

"Yes, three days to get her to Memnope where she belongs," Mark answered, looking at the statue Alexa had placed on the table. The years had rotted away the canvas it had been wrapped in, and bits of dirt still clung to the carved surface.

"She's beautiful," Alexa said as she reached out to touch the sleek golden statue. "Exquisite."

"Yes," Mark agreed. But he seemed to be looking at Alexa rather than the statue. Mark had seen many beautiful art objects in his lifetime, but he'd never known a woman of flesh and blood who could compare with Alexa. He found himself wishing that Aphrodite had never come between them and hoping that she would bring them back together, not move them further apart.

"How will we get her there?" Alexa asked.

Mark looked at her sharply before answering. "I'll have to get to Rhodes and then continue by plane or ferry."

"Ferry would be best," Alexa suggested. "Since Rhodes is the main corridor in and out of the Dodecanese, the Whitfields will probably have someone watching the airport."

Mark nodded. She was getting good at this espionage business, and that bothered him. He didn't want Alexa mixed up in any of it. "That's true, but the ferry doesn't arrive until afternoon. I'd have to get hold of a boat and pick up the ferry at one of the other islands."

"Vassili could take us," Alexa said. "He has a boat, and he knows these waters. He can tell us where the ferries call and when. If we leave right away—"

"What's this 'we,' Alexa?"

"Do you think I'd let you finish this alone?"

"You have no choice."

"Mark—"

"I can't let you risk the danger that could be out there, Alexa."

She wasn't about to give in. "Mark, I'm part of all this. It was my grandfather who took the statue and buried it in the garden. He gave *me* the clue, and I intend to see it through to the end." There was something in her voice, the tilt of her head, the sparkle in her eyes, that told Mark he was going to be asking for trouble if he didn't agree to do as she wanted.

"I'm going with you, and that's all there is to it," she said.

With a sigh, Mark found himself giving in to her, and in spite of the danger, being glad. He wanted her with him. "Go get Vassili," he said, "and I'll pack. We need to get out of here as soon as the sun is up."

Chapter 9

Alexa sat alone at a table in the harborside cafe. Above and behind her the whitewashed houses of Mykonos gleamed in the afternoon sun, and the quaint windmills turned slowly on the occasional whiffs of breeze. Alexa paid no attention.

Along the quay tourists swirled and surged, parading from shop to cafe to shop with no more purpose than to see and be seen in this most fashionable of Greek islands. Alexa hardly noticed them, either. Her eyes as well as her mind were elsewhere.

Far down the quay, Mark stood casually by the dock, his hands pushed into the pockets of his jeans, looking like just another tourist surveying the afternoon scene. He'd been standing there for ten minutes while Alexa tried to figure out what in the world he was doing.

They'd docked half an hour earlier, and Mark had deposited her, along with their gear, at the cafe. Alexa's job was to guard his backpack, her valise and the ominous-looking suitcase. At least it seemed ominous to Alexa, even though it was just the beat-up bag she'd used all through college and then dragged to Greece filled with the books she couldn't bear to leave behind.

Now the suitcase was inches from her foot, and inside was the Aphrodite, which they'd carefully carried with them through the long trip so far. First they'd huddled with it in Vasilli's boat, and then they'd lugged it on to the ferry to Mykonos. The statue had been heavy and Mark had taken charge of it until they'd reached the cafe. There he'd handed it over to Alexa while he went to check the ferries' departure times and pick up their tickets.

That hadn't taken him long. From where she sat Alexa had witnessed the entire transaction. Now she was getting nervous and wished he'd come back and relieve her of the suitcase before she became completely paranoid. She was already beginning to imagine that a man alone at a corner table was eyeing her suspiciously.

Then, as she watched, Mark stepped into a phone booth and closed the door behind him. With a sigh of resignation, Alexa ordered a lemonade and waited, wondering whether he would mention the phone call. If he didn't, she had every intention of asking about it. She was no longer his eager and unwitting accomplice.

Thinking back on their trip together so far, Alexa couldn't help wondering what it might have been like if the Aphrodite had never existed for them. Actually it wouldn't have been any different, Alexa imagined, smiling in spite of herself as she remembered the uncomfortable inter-island ferry. Under the most ideal circumstances, it wouldn't exactly have been a lover's paradise.

No seats had been available below decks so they'd sat outside, trying to protect themselves from the sun and wind and diesel fumes by pulling their deck chairs close to the wheelhouse.

Even if they'd wanted to, it would have been difficult to talk over the clamor of the passengers and the churning engine, but there hadn't been much to say, anyway. Mark had been totally introspective, sitting with his head down, his windbreaker collar turned up against the breeze, lost in his thoughts, seemingly a million miles away.

In spite of the way everything had worked out, Alexa had no qualms about the task she'd undertaken, to return the Aphrodite. She wanted the artifact out of her family's hands and off their consciences. That could only happen when the statue was back where it belonged, in the temple at Memnope. That was the reason, the only reason, Alexa had come along with Mark.

In spite of his promise to return the statue, she had only his word. Right now that didn't count for very much with Alexa. He'd lied to her before.

Even though she'd promised herself to avoid thoughts of what had passed, briefly, between them, Alexa felt the hurt. Yes, he'd lied to her, even if, as he'd said, for a good cause. He'd come to the islands and to Alexa's home with a job to do. She'd made it easy for him.

It was over. They'd been lovers; from now on they'd be partners. Back to the beginning, she thought, sloughing off the hurt that was still there, not about to let it get to her again.

Mark's shadow fell across the table suddenly, and his voice interrupted her thoughts. "You seem very far away."

Alexa looked up with surprise. "I guess I was," she admitted. "Someone could have walked off with the suitcase, and I probably wouldn't have noticed."

Mark laughed. "You'd have noticed, Alexa. Besides, that wasn't my concern. What's troubling you?"

He knew damn well what was troubling her, Alexa thought, angry at herself for being so transparent and determined not to let it happen again. Then she looked over at him as he sat down, reached for her lemonade and took a big swig.

"I'll get you another one," he said with a smile, but there'd been something intimate about his sharing her drink so casually, and once more Alexa was off guard. On top of everything else, the sun was behind him, creating an aureole around his golden hair. She steeled herself again and remembered how deceptive looks could be. After all, wasn't Lucifer the fairest of the angels?

"What about the tickets?" she asked.

Mark didn't seem to notice her tone of voice as he signaled a waiter, ordered two more lemonades and said, "We just barely got onto the 6:00 p.m. ferry. There was only one stateroom left."

Alexa felt herself bristling. "You booked *one* stateroom? I suppose you expect us to share it." From the very beginning, Mark had put her in situations that could lead to intimacy; that much hadn't changed, but this time she was determined not to let his arrangements perturb her.

"I hadn't thought of that," Mark said with a grin, "but I guess it's possible." The waiter deposited two large glasses of lemonade on the table. "However," Mark said after downing half of his in one gulp, "that wasn't my plan. I booked the cabin for you and a seat on deck for myself. Out there in the elements, the spray, the wind . . ."

"Great," Alexa said, reaching for the menu.

"Not even a whit of gratitude for my gentlemanly behavior?"

Alexa shook her head.

"Or guilt that I'll be out in the cold?"

"Nope," she answered. "Shall we order?"

This was the way it should be. She couldn't avoid talking to him, even joking with him, because no matter what had happened they were still on the same wavelength. There was no denying that. But there'd be nothing else between them.

Because the inter-island ferries weren't known for their gourmet food, Mark and Alexa decided on a big meal at the cafe. As they sipped their wine and waited to be served, Mark launched into a long and involved story about the summer of his nineteenth year, which he'd spent on Mykonos.

"It wasn't all devoted to classical studies and archeological digs," he said with something of a leer.

"First there was Sylvie and then Ingrid, and last but not least, Jennifer. And then, after a respite—"

"That's all fascinating, Mark," Alexa said, "but I'm more interested in recent history. For example, the last hour of your life. Here. On the quay."

"The phone call?" he asked.

"The phone call," she answered.

"Well, where should I begin?"

"With the truth."

He glanced at her. Alexa was taking the phone call seriously, and it was up to him to respond accordingly.

"I was planning to tell you later when I had everything figured out," Mark admitted, trying not to sound patronizing. One look at Alexa told him that he hadn't succeeded.

"I've heard that before," she said unsmilingly.

"Alexa, this isn't like before. I wasn't going to take a chance of waiting so long to tell you and have everything backfire." His look was solemn. "I've learned my lesson."

"Just the same," she said, barely listening, "I don't like being brought in at the end. Or have you forgotten?"

"No, I haven't forgotten. How could I forget a mistake that cost me everything we had together?" This time Mark was being serious.

Alexa didn't answer—she *couldn't* answer. It was best for both of them to just let that remark pass.

Mark had a problem, though. As much as he wanted to be honest, he couldn't decide how much to tell her. The more Alexa knew, the more dangerous it would be for her, but at this point in their relationship, not to tell her would be next to impossible. He decided to let her in on everything. Gaining Alexa's trust was important to him now, even though he realized that it might never happen.

"My phone call was to Sir William, who's in the Peloponnisos with the delegation awaiting the ceremony."

"How can they go on with the ceremony when the most important part of the gate is missing?" Alexa's voice registered disbelief.

"They have an Aphrodite."

"Oh?" Alexa looked down at the suitcase beside her.

Mark laughed. "A fake one, a copy derived from drawings made in the 19th century. It hasn't been closely examined yet by the Greeks, but when it is, all hell will break loose. Obviously they know a little something about antiquities," he added.

"Then all we need to do is make a switch," Alexa said. "The real for the fake." She was beginning to get into the spirit of things. "That'll be easy."

"Not quite." Just as Mark answered, the waiter arrived with their meal—plates heaped high with salad, grilled fish and fried potatoes. He poured them each a glass of wine while Alexa waited impatiently.

When the waiter was out of earshot, she asked, "What do you mean by 'not quite?'"

"We can't get to the statue."

"Why not?" she asked, taking a big bite of the fish. "Your godfather will be there. He can give us access to the gate."

"Not when the Greek military has it in safekeeping at the temple where the ceremony will be held."

"Can't Sir William get a key and meet us there?"

Mark shook his head. "Did I tell you that the temple of Aphrodite dates to the fourth century B.C.?" Without pausing for an answer, he explained, "The Bronze Age Mycenaean ruin it rests on dates back fifteen-hundred years earlier." Mark took a few bites to catch up with Alexa, who'd just about finished her fish and was starting on the salad.

"All this intrigue is good for the appetite," he commented.

"Mark," Alexa said impatiently, "please explain what the history lesson has to do with anything."

Mark's response was patiently methodical, almost professorial. "The ruin under Aphrodite's temple is called a *tholos*. It's cyclopean—a huge underground burial chamber made of large, irregular unmortared stones."

Alexa was getting interested. "I've seen photographs of the one at Mycenae."

"There's only one way in, through a guarded entrance and a long tunnel." He took a bite of salad before adding, "It's on military watch around the clock."

Alexa's eyes widened. "They've put the gate underground in the burial chamber?"

"I'm afraid so."

"Then we'll never get to it." Alexa's disappointment was evident.

"You'd really begun to get into this, hadn't you?"

"Yes, I had, and now—"

"There may be a way, Alexa, but it isn't fun and games, I must remind you.

"I realize that, Mark."

"I'm not sure you do. The fate of the Aphrodite is of great political and economic significance. Our government can't afford to have the Greeks find out about the substitute statue and the fact that the British Museum is involved in a scam. On the other hand, we certainly can't afford to get caught making the switch."

Alexa looked at him, waiting.

"That's why I'd like to persuade you to untangle yourself from all this. Stay here on Mykonos until it's all over."

"Not on your life," Alexa exclaimed. "I've come this far on Vasilli's boat and that awful ferry."

"There's one more ferry and an overland trip to go," Mark reminded her.

"Fine. I'm prepared now."

"Failure could be more than embarrassing, Alexa. Soldiers have been known to shoot first and ask questions later. It could be dangerous."

"You're not going to leave me out, Mark Everett. Or Mark Graham. Whatever your name is," Alexa said. "I'm going with you."

Mark held up a shushing hand. "All right, all right."

Satisfied, Alexa dug into the fried potatoes, asking between bites, "What's your plan?"

"Let me give you some background," Mark said. "Sir William and I have roamed that part of the Peloponnisos for years. He even went on a dig at the *tholos*. While he worked, I sailed and swam along the beaches and cliffs. And I found a cave."

Alexa interrupted. "Does it lead to the *tholos*? But won't they have guards there, too?"

"One question at a time," Mark said. "There's a shaft that leads into the chamber. I told Sir William about it, and he has no idea who dug it out. Mycenaeans, maybe, or grave robbers more recently. Anyway, it's there. I imagine a few archeologists know about it, but the military doesn't have an inkling. They're the ones in charge of security."

Alexa sat very still, her face a study in concentration. Finally she spoke, slowly but surely. "We can swim to the cave. That should be easy, just a couple of tourists out for a dip. Once inside, there's no one to see us. We climb up the shaft into the *tholos* and exchange the statues. Before anyone notices, we'll be back swimming in the Aegean."

Mark couldn't help laughing. "I could have used you on a few missions in the past. Your enthusiasm is unbounded. However," he added, "your expertise is nil."

"That doesn't matter," Alexa argued. "It's youth and enthusiasm that counts. That's why all those elderly secret service people are forced to retire and live in the country. They get jaded and start making mistakes. I know. I've read the novels."

Mark was laughing again. "You're right about part of that, Alexa but you're wrong in the main. Enthusiasm can get a person in trouble. True, you climbed the acropolis on Kavos."

"Without looking down," she added.

"This is a cave, Alexa, with a shaft that goes practically straight up."

"I can do it," she said. "Besides, I swim like a fish, and when it comes to partners, I expect I'm in better shape than old Sir William."

"Of that there's no doubt," Mark said, taking a sip of wine.

"As for the shaft, that'll be no problem."

"Oh?"

"It's dark in there. As long as there's nothing to look down on, I won't know how high up I am."

"Whatever you say, Alexa." Mark realized that he couldn't talk her out of it now. "There's another problem, however, one that's much more dangerous."

Alexa looked up, alarmed. She had managed to gird herself for the job ahead, knowing it wouldn't be easy, but she was no fool. Danger didn't appeal to her at all.

"Your good friends Charlotte and Tony."

"Mark, are you sure they're after the Aphrodite?"

"I haven't the slightest doubt."

"But why? What do they have to gain?"

"I don't know that yet, Alexa. Maybe they want to create an international incident, embarrass both countries to the delight of whatever government they're working for. Or," he added, "they could just be in it for the money, for themselves."

"But they're already wealthy," Alexa objected.

"How do you think they got that way?"

"As thieves?"

Mark just shrugged.

Alexa's cabin on the ferry was no bigger than a closet. Two narrow bunks were stacked against one wall; on the other was, in succession, a porthole, the hall door and the bathroom door. Under the porthole was a table and a straight chair.

Mark had deposited her luggage on the floor and was looking around, grinning.

"Perfect for Lilliputians," Alexa had commented.

"Sleep well, Alexa," he'd said, taking the suitcase and his backpack and disappearing down the hall.

After he left, Alexa undressed, brushed her teeth at the minuscule basin in the bathroom, cursed the pathetic flow of lukewarm water and ran a brush through her hair. Now she lay in the bed staring at the mattress of the bunk above her. Not very exciting or adventurous. Certainly not very romantic. She managed to turn that last thought off. She wasn't on this trip for romance, and espionage was often unexciting, she remembered from the spy novels.

She turned on the overhead light, but it was too dim to read by even if she'd thought to bring a book. As it was, all she had was the local newspaper, which she had difficulty reading in the best of light. She tossed it aside.

A fitful, damp breeze blew in through the porthole, bringing with it the odor of diesel fuel and fish. The ferry was delivering a fresh catch to customers in the Peloponnisos. There was also the underlying faint smell of rain.

She turned off the light and sank back against her hard pillow, wishing she could sleep. A pinging sound against the porthole kept her wide awake. Finally, Alexa sat up in bed and looked out. It was raining, but it was just a little squall, she told herself, that would pass soon. It never rained in Greece in the summer. At the same time, she knew that they were far from land and could easily be in the track of a storm blowing in from the Mediterranean.

Then she knew it wasn't the sound of the rain that was keeping her awake. It was the thought of Mark out on deck.

"Serves him right," she murmured aloud, remembering that he liked to sleep outside. But that didn't help. Finally after tossing and turning for another half hour, Alexa gave up. As long as he was outside in the rain, she would be wide awake. It was for herself more than for him that she was giving in to her conscience, Alexa decided as she got up and pulled on jeans, sandals and a windbreaker.

Upstairs in the lounge she was confronted by a scene straight out of Dante's *Inferno*. Sleeping hordes of men, women and children lay sprawled on couches and chairs, some rolled up in their coats on the floor. Babies cried as children no more than three years old played tag among the sleeping forms, oblivious to the noise. Someone had been seasick, and the stench drove Alexa outside.

There the air was clean, but the rain had turned into a penetrating drizzle that coated the deck, the chairs and the few passengers still topside. Slowly Alexa moved from chair to chair, peering into sleeping faces.

"*Oriste*?" A dark, mustachioed man rose up suddenly and confronted her as she moved among the deck chairs.

"Sorry, sorry. Excuse me." In her embarrassment, Alexa forgot her Greek entirely. Backing away, she almost ran right into Mark.

His chair was pulled up next to an overhang. He'd commandeered a blanket from somewhere, but it was coated with a combination of rain and sea spray.

"Mark," she whispered, "wake up."

His blue eyes popped open, and from the mischievous expression in them Alexa had a feeling he'd been lying there watching her progress across the deck.

"I'm not asleep, Alexa," he said. "Only ducks can sleep in the rain."

"Then why don't you come downstairs?"

"Into your stateroom?" he asked with just a touch of pomposity.

"There's no reason to be sarcastic, Mark," she responded. "Just come. I'm getting wet, too."

"Well, we can't have that," Mark said as he followed her across the deck.

Alexa briefly considered retracting her offer but decided to ignore him instead. They made their way down the corridor and into her cabin.

The tiny room seemed even smaller now as Mark stooped over and stepped inside. He wasn't just tall; he was overpowering, filling the room.

He put the suitcase in the corner and dropped his backpack on top of it almost casually. When he stepped away he was facing Alexa. There was just enough room for the two of them and the luggage.

"Okay," he said. "Here we are."

He was so close Alexa could see the raindrops glistening in his hair and eyebrows. His face had a shine to it, a dampness that made her want to reach out and touch him. Quickly she stepped away, only to feel the doorknob jab her in the back. There was no room for retreat.

Worse than that, there was nowhere to look but straight at Mark. She met the mocking look in his eyes and remembered that from the first moment she'd met him, he'd enjoyed throwing her off balance, making her blush and feel uncomfortable.

Yet she didn't really feel uncomfortable; that was the problem. She could very easily have fallen under the spell of Mark's charms again. She knew that, and so did he as he stood only inches away, his chest rising and falling with each easy breath.

"So what do we do next?" he persisted. "I'm game for anything." A slow smile curved his lips.

Alexa smiled back, feigning an ease that she didn't really feel but determined not to let him know about her nerves. "First," she said calmly, "I'll get undressed, into bed and out of your way. Then you can do... well, whatever you want."

"Shall I close my eyes while you undress?"

"Since I'll be in the bathroom, I don't think that's necessary," she answered coolly.

Mark just smiled and watched as she turned sideways and eased herself into the bathroom, grabbing her gown that hung on the door as she passed.

He was still standing in the same place when Alexa emerged and slid under the sheets. "Okay," she said. "It's all yours now."

Mark didn't show any inclination to go into the bathroom, and realizing this, Alexa turned over so that she was facing the wall and could only imagine what was happening in the room as he undressed.

She heard the whoosh of his zipper as he took off his windbreaker and then tossed it onto the chair. She suspected that he was unbuttoning his shirt now, but couldn't be sure. Then she heard the sound of his jeans being unsnapped, another whisper of a zipper followed by the rustle of cloth sliding down his legs. She wondered if he wore anything under his jeans. All she had to do was look, but she was careful not to since she was sure by now Mark was completely naked.

When she heard him rummaging in his backpack, Alexa couldn't resist one peek. She turned over, opened her eyes for a split second and caught a glimpse of long, tanned legs and taut, white rear. Just as quickly she closed her eyes again.

"Sorry to make so much noise. Got to brush my teeth."

"It's okay," she whispered. Her throat was tight and dry, and she felt her face start to burn.

Mark was completely unconscious of his body—Alexa knew that. From the very first she'd been totally aware of him. That couldn't change in spite of the shift in their relationship. She managed to turn again and face the wall, breathing a sigh of relief that it was all over.

Yet it wasn't. She heard the bathroom door close and then open again, and for a moment he came and stood by the bunk beds. Alexa held her breath, hoping he wouldn't reach for her, touch her, because if he did she knew that she would respond.

Making love wouldn't change anything; it certainly wouldn't restore the trust she'd lost. It would only complicate their lives.

But he didn't reach for her. Instead, he flicked off the light and hoisted himself into the upper bunk. It groaned and swayed for a moment beneath his weight, but held. After a few minutes, he settled himself in, and then everything was still.

"Good night, Alexa," he said quietly.

She lay silently in the dark.

* * *

Mark was waiting for her on deck the next morning, two cups of steaming coffee on the little table by his deck chair. She took one gratefully.

"Our destination is ahead," he said, "the Peloponnisos, and specifically the seaport where I hope we can pick up a rental car."

"I don't suppose there'll be any time to explore," she said regretfully.

"Only the shops. While I see what I can rent in the way of a car for the drive to Memnope, you can hit the shops and..." He paused and grimaced. "Damn, this is going to sound melodramatic."

"What?" Alexa pressed. "Guns? Ammunition?"

Mark threw back his head and laughed. "Now, that's *really* melodramatic. I was going to say disguises. If Tony and Charlotte are in the area, we'll have to give them a run for their money and not make finding us so easy."

"Do you think they could have figured out our route and turned up here?"

"I doubt it," Mark answered. "Obviously they know our ultimate destination. They'll try to stop us in Memnope." He noticed the expression on her face, but more than that he noticed her shadowed eyes, how tired she looked.

"Listen, Alexa," he said gently, "there's still time for you to get out of this. I can handle it alone from here."

Alexa took a bracing sip of coffee. "I'm in this all the way, Mark," she said. "Now tell me what you mean by disguises? Wigs, funny noses..."

Mark laughed. "I don't think we have to go that far, Alexa. We just need something that will enable us to blend into the crowd. Something different from what they've seen us in, clothes that are more continental, a wig, maybe. Tinted glasses like the Europeans wear."

Alexa nodded enthusiastically. "I have the picture. Where shall I meet you?"

"In the main square. There's a statue that you can't miss. I'll pick you up as soon as I get hold of a rental car." He looked at his watch. "Say an hour after we dock."

Mark was sitting on a stone bench feeding scraps of pastry to a friendly pigeon when Alexa arrived, carrying two big shopping bags.

"I did great," she bragged.

He thrust a paper bag at her. "Pastries. Have one before the birds get them all."

She chose a powdered-sugar-covered object that she couldn't identify. It looked flaky and delicious.

"I think it's filled with rum," he told her.

"All the better," Alexa said, taking a bite.

"I'd better tell you the bad news now," Mark said. "Our car, if we want it, is in Tripolis."

Alexa sank down beside him, her face filled with disbelief. "In North Africa?" she asked, astounded.

Mark had to laugh. "It's bad, Alexa, but not quite that bad. Tripolis, Greece, not Tripoli. It's a few kilometers east. The car was supposed to be returned here, but the tourists who rented it dropped it off in Tripolis."

"There're no other cars available?" Alexa didn't know why she was asking when she knew the answer.

"It's a busy tourist time. Anything that's running is out on the road."

Alexa nibbled at the pastry. "Okay," she said. "What's next?"

Mark looked at her in amazement. She didn't seem upset in the slightest. "You're certainly taking this all in stride."

"I never thought it would be easy," she responded. "Frankly a missing car in the whole scheme of things hardly seems like a real problem." Alexa thought back over the past few days and what they'd been through and gave him a big smile that showed her enthusiasm.

Spontaneously Mark reached for her with a quick hug. "Good girl."

Once he had her in his arms, he didn't want to let go, and for a moment he held on, and she didn't resist.

He'd treated her shabbily, lied to her, misled her, and now here she was, enthusiastically sticking by him. Mark couldn't get over that. And yet it wasn't enough for him. He wanted now what he'd wanted all along, her love. In losing that, he'd lost everything.

Mark thought about the night before in that tacky little cabin below deck. If everything had been good between them, that could have been a wonderful night of love with the rain pounding against the porthole and he and Alexa wrapped in each other's arms.

But everything hadn't been right. He'd taken care of that a long time before with his lies to her that she wasn't about to forgive.

As he held her tighter, Mark felt Alexa stiffen in his arms. He wasn't surprised by her reaction, and he quickly stepped away, but not without taking out his handkerchief and wiping the sugary tart crumbs from her lips.

Looking down at her, Mark got lost for a moment in the golden flakes that sparkled in her dark eyes. He wet his lips, aching to kiss her right there in the square and feel the smoothness of her skin, the softness of her mouth. He'd wanted her last night; he wanted her even more now.

Alexa saw the look in his eyes and moved away, brushing her hair from her face, smiling at him, but putting space between them.

"I guess we'd better hit the road," she said. "We still have some traveling to do."

Mark nodded. The moment had passed, and once more he and Alexa were partners on the road to Memnope.

Chapter 10

Alexa sank back in the tub of sudsy water. A bliss-ful smile played over her face as she stretched her tired muscles luxuriously. The little hotel in Tripolis, al-though hardly deluxe, was a much-needed refuge from recent events.

Their overland trip had started off well enough. The battered but apparently operable bus had left on schedule, and Alexa had been able to make a pillow of her jacket, curl up on a seat and fall into a somewhat fitful sleep.

It was during that sleep that the bus gave a sudden shuddering lurch and then came to a thudding stop. Alexa, nearly thrown off the seat, pulled herself up-right and brushed her hair out of her tired eyes. "What—"

"A flat tire, probably," Mark assured her from

across the aisle. "I'll see if I can give the driver a hand."

Suddenly the bus seemed to come alive as the passengers reacted to the accident as if it were a special, exciting event to be observed and commented on by all. The male contingent, except for one elderly and possibly blind gnome of a man seated in the back, followed Mark outside to offer their advice and assistance.

The women leaned out of the windows on Alexa's side of the bus, chattering excitedly. In the back a baby began to cry as its mother tried vainly to soothe it, finally gave up and leaned out of her window, too, more interested in what was going on outside than in.

Even Alexa couldn't resist a peek through the dusty glass, but all that she could see were the men standing at the rear of the bus, arguing with the driver who gestured wildly and then threw up his arms in frustration.

Finally Mark clambered back into the bus and settled beside her. "Flat tire as I suspected. We've landed in a ditch, but there should be no problem lifting the bus out."

"So we won't be long," Alexa ventured, stretching her arms high over her head to work out the kinks in her neck and shoulders.

"Well," Mark began, "that might be true if we had a good spare, but unfortunately it's flat, too."

Alexa stifled a groan. "This can't be happening."

"Don't worry. The driver is optimistic."

Alexa joined in Mark's immediate laughter. "I noticed, but I'm afraid he doesn't exactly have the respect of his passengers."

"No, but he is equipped with a certain amount of resilience. He plans to flag a passing lorry, get a ride back to town and pick up a new tire."

Alexa heaved a sigh. The passengers had just about all piled out of the bus and were lolling around at the side of the road. "They don't look like they expect success in this venture."

"But they don't look like they care, either," Mark observed. "I suggest you follow their example. There's a grove of orange trees up there on the hill. You can relax and continue your nap. This shouldn't take more than a couple of hours."

His calculation was off by another two and a half hours, during which Alexa managed to keep her spirits up, but by the time they reached Tripolis, she was showing her exhaustion.

Mark picked up their rental car, but after one look at Alexa, who'd fallen asleep on his shoulder before he got out of the parking lot, he decided not to drive on.

"It's not the best road under ideal circumstances," he explained. "I don't know this car so I can't predict whether or not it'll survive the trip. However, I'm pretty sure that you won't."

Alexa tried to object, but he would have none of it. "Besides," Mark told her, "too many cars and lorries travel at night without lights. I'd feel safer if we waited until daybreak." Then he smiled down at her tenderly. "I think we both deserve a hot bath and a soft bed."

Alexa could barely keep awake long enough to nod in agreement.

After a nap, she was refreshed enough to give some thought to cleaning up and eating dinner, in that order. First she washed her hair and then spent far too long in the old-fashioned tub, regretfully emerging when the water began to cool. She had twenty minutes to get herself ready and meet Mark in the lobby downstairs.

She took an hour, but as far as Mark was concerned, the wait was worth it. And it gave him time to find a good hiding place for the statue. When she entered the lobby, Alexa looked like herself again, fresh and beautiful. He would have waited even longer for the chance to spend an evening with her.

And it was an evening to remember. The restaurant that the desk clerk recommended was small, family-run, quiet, unpretentious and exceptional. As predicted, the *souvlaki* was particularly good, the salad fresh and crisp, and the dessert pastries buttery beyond belief.

Alexa ate every bite of food, responding to Mark's comments and observations monosyllabically between bites.

Finally she pushed back her plate and sighed. "That was wonderful."

"Obviously this restaurant is the one bright spot in Tripolis. Otherwise, the chief attraction seems to be the bus station."

Alexa smiled. "Kind of a sad little town, but if there had to be one good spot, I'm glad this is it. Besides," she added, "the hotel is clean and comfortable and paradise to my tired bones."

"Too tired for coffee and Metaxa?"

"Never," she answered. "I'd like to unwind a little more."

"Good," Mark said. "That'll give us a chance to talk."

"About how we'll replace the statue? That's been on my mind a great deal recently. I know there're certain things that can't be planned, but—"

"That's not what I meant, Alexa," Mark interrupted almost curtly. He already knew what lay ahead, and he'd given it as much consideration as was necessary. Then he'd allowed time to turn completely unprofessional and think about Alexa. And himself.

"I'm talking about us," he said slowly, watching her eyes as he spoke. "And what happened on Kavos."

Alexa couldn't stop the quickening of her heart or prevent the dryness in her throat, but she managed to sit quietly while Mark signaled the waiter, who brought their coffee and brandy.

She knew the silence had to be broken, and that meant dragging out all the painful and confusing feelings that had been aired briefly but incompletely before. Or letting them lie. Walking away.

Mark watched as she sipped her coffee. There were any number of possibilities available to her now, but he could only hope that she would give in to the powerful need for both of them to purge themselves of what had happened and not to ignore it. No matter what the outcome was, he deserved a hearing.

She knew that. "I guess it's now or never."

"Yes," he agreed and then couldn't think where to go from there. He'd already explained what had come before, the sequence of events that had put him on Kavos and, ultimately, into her arms. What remained for him was to try to explain his feelings.

"I didn't mean to take advantage of you," he said awkwardly. "Good Lord, I *didn't* take advantage of you, Alexa. We're both adults. We were attracted to each other, and that had nothing to do with my job."

"No?"

"No," he said vehemently. "You have to believe that or the rest is pointless. I cared for you. I still do." He looked her steadily in the eye. "Do you believe me, Alexa?"

She nodded, unable to deny the feelings that were so strong and true between them.

"When we made love—"

Alexa turned away.

"No, look at me, Alexa," he demanded. "When we made love, there was more between us than passion. There was a wonder, a caring."

"Then why didn't you tell me the truth?" she cried. "Why did you keep that lie between us?"

It was Mark's turn to look away. "Because I wanted what we had to continue," he said, staring out into the now-empty restaurant. "I wanted to hold on to what I'd found."

"But you knew that wasn't possible," Alexa said bluntly.

Mark could only nod in agreement, still avoiding her eyes.

"You have a career that doesn't leave room for relationships." It wasn't a question; it was a simple statement of facts. Mark was an agent, committed to his country and his job. This search for Aphrodite had been a diversion, almost a vacation for him. When it was over, he would return to where he really belonged. And she certainly didn't belong there with him. Kavos was home for Alexa now.

But she couldn't deny what had happened between them. The circumstances no longer mattered. The feelings were there even if she had no future with Mark.

"When this is over, you'll be going back to England," she said. As she waited for his response, knowing full well that it would be affirmative, Alexa couldn't resist a glimmer of hope, but it faded quickly.

"Yes," he said firmly, not wanting to give fruitless hope to either of them. "And you'll be staying on Kavos."

Sometime while they'd been talking, he'd reached out and covered her hand with his. She felt an added pressure now, and it gave her strength.

"Before that happens," he said, "before I leave, I want everything to be good between us, and that can't come about until you forgive me for everything, the lies, the tricks."

Somewhere inside of her, Alexa had already forgiven him.

"When we say goodbye, I want everything to be right with us," he pleaded.

"It will be," she promised.

Mark felt his breath return, faster than before. It seemed as if he'd been holding it all that time, waiting for her forgiveness. It would all be easier now. Even though he didn't want to think ahead to the time when they had to say goodbye, at least he could face it.

"If you ever believe anything," he said, "believe this. What happened was real and true. For me."

"And for me," Alexa said. Everything was forgiven. More than that, it was forgotten. With her relief came a momentary glimmer of tears. She fought them back, but the moment was so heavy with emotion that Alexa had to look away. This wasn't the time to cry. They were friends again but no more than that.

She slipped her hand from his and picked up the glass of brandy, trying to smile. At first it wasn't possible; there was just too much deep feeling churning inside her. But at last she managed to control her emotions. Another sip of brandy helped; her smile emerged.

Alexa was happy to see an answering grin in return.

"Maybe this leopard can change his spots," Mark said.

"Do you mean it's possible for an old dog to learn new tricks?" she teased, responding to his axiom with one equally as trite, glad that the mood had lightened.

"Well, let's not go that far," he answered with another grin as he finished his brandy and then looked at the empty glass almost with regret. "There's no better way to end a perfect meal."

"Both the dinner and the brandy were exceptional," Alexa agreed.

"Do you think it's possible that they were further enhanced by our being together?"

When Alexa answered only with a half-smile that he couldn't interpret, Mark gave her hand a quick squeeze and said, "We'd better be getting back to the hotel. Our day will start awfully early tomorrow."

They walked in silence through the quiet streets, their footsteps echoing hollowly in the night. Mark thought about taking her hand, but changed his mind just before he reached out. She might pull away, and he didn't want that. Besides, they were very close without touching. For Mark it was almost as if he were holding her. That would be enough for now.

The silence prevailed as they crossed the hotel lobby and climbed the stairs to Alexa's room; the mood was the same, too. To speak would be to end it.

Mark took the key from her hand, unlocked the door, pushed it open and turned on the light. The room wasn't helped by illumination. Quickly he reached out and flicked on the bedside lamp.

"It might be a good idea to turn off the overhead," he advised. "This place doesn't fare too well in direct light."

The double bed and sagging mattress, peeling wallpaper and lopsided bureau looked so sad and forlorn that Alexa had to laugh.

"It's clean, and that's all that matters. I wouldn't sleep any better in a five-star hotel."

"Which is what you deserve," Mark said. "I'm afraid this has been a hell of a trip."

"I'm not complaining," Alexa answered.

"I know you're not, and that makes it even harder for me."

Mark was standing beside the bed. He forced himself to step away, but he couldn't leave. Nothing, no one in the world could make him leave. Except Alexa.

He waited.

She looked up at him hesitantly, but not without a sort of expectation—at least that was how Mark interpreted it. He could no more leave her than he could take his eyes off her. Her lips were parted slightly, and he told himself that was what seemed expectant about her. Yet it could also have been the slight frown that played across her forehead. Or the flush in her cheeks.

He raised his hand and touched her soft, dark hair. She was so still and silent that she seemed almost unreal. But the warmth of her skin as the back of his hand brushed her cheek was very, very real, and it filled him with desire.

He meant to be gentle, not to hurry her or frighten her with the strength of his need. But while he managed to control his hands, he couldn't stop the words from escaping his lips. "Alexa," he said huskily, "I want you so..."

She tried to answer, but her voice caught in her throat, and she could only respond with her eyes.

That was enough for Mark. All the feelings that he'd kept in check were set free at last. His lips were on hers, and he was kissing her as if for the first time, as if for the last.

Alexa filled his arms, invaded his senses and set him afire. Somehow he managed to reach out and push the door closed. Then they were alone in a strangely charming room in an out of the way Greek town, and it was suddenly paradise.

"I want to stay with you tonight," he whispered.

"Yes," Alexa answered softly.

"You won't send me away?"

"No, no," she cried out. "Not tonight. I've missed you too much."

Mark cupped her face in his hands and kissed her again and again. "I'm sorry, so sorry. I never meant to hurt you, never, never—"

"I know," she said.

At last. Mark felt a sigh of relief escape his lips as his hands found the buttons on her blouse, the zipper on her skirt. He heard them fall in a soft whisper to the floor, and then he felt her in his arms, warm and vibrant and alive.

"Your clothes," she murmured. His shirt was rubbing against her tender breasts.

"Yes, I—" He fumbled with his buttons, but her hands stopped him.

Alexa seemed to be laughing at him, as if amused by his awkwardness. And he did feel awkward, like a schoolboy.

Her fingers were quick, and in less than a moment she was sliding his shirt off his shoulders, reaching for the snap of his jeans. Then their bodies were touching. His chest, his abdomen, his thighs pressed hard against her. And so did his arousal; Mark wished he could be more subtle, wished he could control himself, but he couldn't, not for Alexa. His body revealed his need.

He gathered her to him and lay down with her on the bed. "I want this to be the first time for us," he said.

"It will be." Alexa knew what he meant. It would be the first time that they would make love honestly. There would be no lies, no deceptions. They'd seen the worst of each other; now they would *be* the best.

"This will be perfect," he promised, his lips lingering on hers, his hands eagerly roaming her body.

"You'll forget the Mark you knew before," he said in a voice that begged rather than commanded.

Her response surprised him.

Looking up with wide, dark eyes, Alexa whispered, "There were some things about that Mark I liked. I don't want to forget *them*." As if to explain, her hands touched his body in all the places that excited her, moving along the muscles of his chest and back, over his buttocks and around, holding him close with one hand while her other continued to explore greedily.

With each touch she fed the flame that consumed him.

"Oh, Alexa," he managed to whisper. "All I want is to make you happy, and I will, I will."

It was his turn to prove his words and spread the flame from his body to hers. His lips slid across her cheek to her chin and down the smooth column of her neck. He found the soft, sweet place behind her ear and kissed her until she trembled and her nails dug into his back.

But Mark had only begun. His lips moved to the valley between her breasts and then to one tempting nipple. His tongue played, tantalized, flicked as Alexa dissolved beneath his touch. Deep within she felt a passion consuming her like a white-hot coil, tightening, tightening inside.

The passion intensified as his lips moved lower, his teeth grazing the line of her hipbone, his lips tasting the salty softness of her inner thigh, his tongue at last discovering her honeyed sweetness.

The coil inside expanded and twisted, and without knowing it Alexa began to writhe under his touch, head flung back, eyes closed, giving herself up to sensation.

It was torture; it was heaven. A delirium possessed her for which there was no letup, no relief. She couldn't speak, could hardly breathe. It was all she had ever wanted and more than she could bear. Then, when the fiery tension within her became unbearable, she was released and felt herself explode into a thousand starry fragments.

Mark was cradling her, his cheek against her abdomen, his arms beneath her, holding tight. She ran her hands through his hair as he moved up her body until his lips found hers.

Before Alexa's head had stopped swimming from the joy of what had just happened, she felt the need rise within her again as his lips and tongue and teeth met hers and his flesh grew hot and pliant against her.

Then he was inside her, strong and hard, and it began again, more powerful than before. That had been the prelude; this was the symphony.

They moved together just as she remembered, in harmony, in perfect rhythm. He was part of her and she of him. They were one.

Alexa clung to his shoulders. They were so damp and slippery she could hardly hold him close enough. She wrapped her legs around his back and lifted her body upward. As he held her she could hear the pounding of his heart and then there was a release, a joyous moment when they both let go. Together they found that perfect place that was at first delirium, and then, suddenly, peace.

He held her for a long, long time, not wanting to ever let her go. When at last she started to move away, he said, "No, please stay beside me, Alexa."

His hand smoothed her hair, and Alexa sighed, putting her cheek against his shoulder. It felt good to be held by Mark; it felt warm and safe and secure. They had made love freely and wonderfully, and the bitterness that had been between them before had fled. What remained was a feeling so perfect and complete that Alexa could only fear it because she knew it wouldn't last.

He knew it, too, and that was why he wanted her to stay close. For that moment, for that night at least, they would be together as one. Tomorrow was another day, and not to be thought of now in this lovely darkness that held them in such perfect peace.

For a moment when she'd nearly slipped away, Alexa had felt him grow tense, almost afraid, and she'd known not to leave him, not even to move inches away because inches were like miles from him tonight. She would stay close and like Mark she wouldn't talk of the future, wouldn't even think of it. She would lie until dawn's light in his arms and hold him as he held her.

She wanted only the beat of his heart and the rhythm of his breathing, only the touch of his moist skin against hers. She wanted to push back the damp curls of his hair, run her fingers along his cheek and feel the faint stubble of his beard. She wanted to fall asleep in his arms and wake in his arms and not think about Aphrodite or Sir William or the ceremony or the Whitfields.

And she got what she wanted, at least for now, for tonight, falling asleep with the wish in her heart that the trouble between them had never begun and the wish that their time together would never end.

They arrived in Memnope at noon. The trip across the mountains from Tripolis in the light of day hadn't been dangerous, only tiring, with frequent detours further aggravated by traffic jams created by carloads of tourists pouring in from Italy and Yugoslavia.

Alexa was disappointed with the town. It was barely more attractive than Tripolis, although it did boast a seacoast, which Mark assured her was quite lovely.

"Where?" she'd asked.

"North of here," he'd told her. "And there's a harbor that's very appealing."

Alexa was a little doubtful, but she didn't dwell on the lack of scenic attractiveness in Memnope. They weren't there for the view.

They pulled up to a small commercial hotel on the outskirts of town. Mark stopped her as she reached for the car door.

"I think it would be best for me to register alone this time, Alexa. I have no doubt the Whitfields are in town looking for us and our passenger." He nodded toward the invisible but carefully wrapped statue hidden away in Alexa's suitcase.

Alexa was silent and thoughtful for a while before responding with a question. "Then how are we going to work this? The Whitfields know your name, too. Unless—"

Mark had let her go on, waiting to see where her thoughts led. "Unless?" he asked with mock näiveté.

Alexa pushed her dark glasses up on her hair. "Is this some kind of spy stuff?"

Mark laughed, not altogether amused. "I do just happen to have a passport in the name of a West German citizen, Herr Jurgen Dettwald."

"Well, that's fine for you, Mark, but having no assumed name and therefore unable to register with you, what's the scenario for me—spending the night in our rental car?"

He leaned across the seat and kissed her. "Do you really think I would let you do that?"

"I'm not sure how an agent's mind works," she responded semiseriously. "But I assume you have a plan."

"Naturally," he answered. "I'll register as Herr Dettwald and send the bellboy out for the luggage. All of it," he added, "including yours."

"That's big of you," Alexa said. "What happens next, now that my things are in your room and I'm still in the car?" In spite of Alexa's carefully blasé attitude, she was beginning to feel excitement building inside her.

"You glance around casually, and then emerge from the car. A few more provocative looks and you unobtrusively stroll through the hotel lobby and up to our room."

"Like one of the local ladies of the night?"

"Now, that's your suggestion, Alexa, but since you mention it—"

"Mark!" Then she grinned. "I like it," she declared. "I've never even been close to a lady of the night, much less masqueraded as one. Let's see," she said, ticking off their recent experiences on her fingers. "Since meeting you I've found buried treasure, had my house vandalized, fled from supposed international thieves and traveled across Greece on a bus with a flat spare tire—"

"Which just happened to have a blowout."

"Only figures," Alexa nodded.

Mark kissed her lightly on the nose. "You ain't seen nothing yet," he declared. "Now, get out of the car and lurk attractively—as if you could lurk any other way—over there near the corner. I'll be out soon with the bellboy."

Alexa climbed from the car and crossed the street, trying to move unnoticed among the stands that sold sandals, T-shirts, cutlery and a hodgepodge of household and tourist items.

She was busily admiring a hand-painted pottery saucer when she saw Mark reappear. He gave instructions for unloading the baggage and waited until the bellboy had gone back into the hotel before turning toward her with a wide grin. He held up four fingers and then three.

Alexa turned her back as if she hadn't seen him. If this was any indication of his secret agent's abilities, he was being eminently cavalier, she decided. After waiting about ten minutes and finally buying a pair of sandals from the shop's proprietor, who was becoming suspicious over her loitering, Alexa crossed the street.

She avoided the lobby, instead turned into an alley that ran alongside the hotel. Just as she'd suspected, there was a door marked Deliveries. She slipped inside, pausing a moment to let her eyes adjust to the half-light before walking up the short flight of stairs to the lobby level.

Once there, Alexa stopped again, her hand on the door. Should she take the chance of walking through to the elevators? Creating an imaginary scenario, she found herself being stopped by a suspicious desk clerk. She conjured up a few questions to which she had no answers and decided to walk rather than chancing the confrontation.

Four flights later, breathing hard, Alexa located room 43. Mark opened it at her first faint knock.

"You couldn't get a room on the second floor?" she gasped.

"Not one this nice," he responded, ushering her in.

Alexa looked around and was pleasantly surprised. The room had a large and comfortable-looking double bed with a bright quilted cover, tiled floors, an immaculate and very modern bath and even a tiny balcony overlooking a pocket-size but verdant garden.

"I thought we deserved something better than the ferry or Tripolis for our last stop."

Last stop. The words echoed in Alexa's brain, reminding her of something she'd almost forgotten. Certainly she'd wanted to forget it, but she needed the reminder. Alexa was sure that Mark realized that.

They were on borrowed time. Inadvertently she glanced at her watch. Barely twenty-four hours until the ceremony.

He put his hand over the face of her watch. At first Alexa thought he'd meant to stop the time for them, but then she realized it wasn't a symbolic gesture as he turned her wrist over, brought it to his lips and placed a kiss there beside the pale blue vein.

He looked at her silently for a long moment. There was nothing to say; their future was determined, and only the details of their last adventure needed reviewing.

When he let go of her hand, Alexa smoothed back her hair with casual nonchalance and asked, "So, what's on the agenda?"

Mark dropped down onto the bed and arranged himself comfortably, long legs crossed, hands behind his head. Alexa could only wonder if the casualness was there to cover up his feelings. She didn't have time to decide. "We need to reconnoiter," Mark said, "to check out the temple and the *tholos*..."

"By car?" She asked, sitting down beside him and assuming the same easy attitude.

"Nope, I don't think so. We'll go by sea since that's how we'll be entering the temple tonight. And I need to reconfirm some of my boyhood memories, see if they're still accurate."

"What's our m.o.?" Alexa asked.

Mark threw his head back and laughed. "You're really into this, aren't you? Modus operandi, eh? I'd say it's time for the disguises."

"Great," Alexa said. "I hoped all my shopping wouldn't be in vain."

Mark knew as well as Alexa that this was the end of things, but he also knew that it didn't have to end with her facing danger. His feelings for her were no less strong than they'd ever been; his concern for her was even stronger. He took her hand again, and this time he didn't plan to release it.

"Alexa," he said with determination. "I want you to stay here—"

"We settled that earlier, Mark."

"I know, but—"

"Please, Mark. I'm going with you."

For one brief and beautiful moment, he was holding her, and she was sure that their thoughts were the same—not of the ceremony ahead but of something, somewhere for the two of them.

Mark had also experienced a brief moment dwelling in a dreamworld that they could inhabit together, but he overcame it with a toughness he'd learned from years of experience assessing and analyzing facts, not dreaming, never dreaming.

He squeezed her tightly one more time and gave her bottom a pat. "Come on, partner," he said. "We need to get going." Mark threw his legs over the side of the bed. "Herr and Frau Dettwald are about to charter themselves a boat."

The couple were obviously tourists. The man did most of the talking in heavily accented English while his wife threw in a few badly pronounced Greek words for clarification.

He wore white cotton pants, a printed shirt and shiny new deck shoes. His light-colored hair was concealed under a jaunty sailor's cap. She was as blond as he, but had tied her hair back securely with a scarf. Huge dark glasses hid her eyes. She was wearing brightly flowered stretch pants and a tight-fitting T-shirt. Local fishermen lounging near their boats made appreciative sounds as she walked past.

Finally the couple were able to locate just the boat they wanted and come to terms with the fisherman who owned it. He agreed to take them snorkeling out near Aphrodite's temple and for an additional fee to rent them snorkeling gear.

The couple seemed pleased, and the man willingly peeled off a large wad of bills. Their bargain struck, the man helped his wife into the bobbing craft. Over the cries of the gulls and the roar of the motor, no one could hear him as he bent near and whispered to her.

"Over your left shoulder, in the white yacht riding at anchor. Our friends are here."

Chapter 11

After returning to the harbor and docking their boat, Alexa and Mark walked along the quay toward the hotel. Alexa could feel her heart pounding, and the palms of her hands were clammy. This was going to be the hard part. What had come before was easy.

They'd escaped the Whitfields by turning the boat around and heading out toward the open sea. Once out of view of the Whitfields' yacht, Mark had doubled back so they could have a look at the temple in preparation for the night ahead.

When they docked two hours later, the Whitfields' boat was riding at anchor in the harbor. "They're somewhere in Memnope," Alexa said.

"A good guess," Mark replied with a grin.

"It's not funny, Mark. You're a real spy. I'm only a novice, and I'm scared. What if we see them? Worse, what if they see us?"

"Obviously they're looking for us so we can lead them back to the hotel and the Aphrodite. So that's exactly what we have to avoid."

They moved quickly across the quay and approached the street that wound along the waterfront. It was crowded with shops, and there were tourists everywhere. Once they reached the street, it was only a few yards to the taxis. One would take them back to the hotel where they could stay hidden until the night brought a blessed cover of darkness.

Only one more short block and they would be at the street. Already a driver at the head of the line had jumped out of his car and flung open the door expectantly.

"We've almost made it," Alexa whispered.

She'd barely spoken the words when the pressure on her arm suddenly increased. "There they are," Mark said. "In the cafe having coffee. Don't look at them and just keep on walking."

Alexa felt as though her feet had turned to lead. It was a Herculean task to lift one in front of the other. Part of her wanted to stop and part to run. She was tempted to turn her head and look at Charlotte and Tony but knew she didn't dare.

"They won't recognize us," Mark reminded her. "Stay cool."

"Easy for you to say." Alexa was trying to joke, but her throat was tight and dry, and her heart beat heavily in her chest.

They drew near the table where Tony and Charlotte were sitting at the open-air cafe. Neither seemed to notice the passersby, Alexa determined as she let out the breath she'd been holding.

At the moment relief flooded over her, Tony and Charlotte pushed back their chairs and got up from the table. Tony flung down some bills to cover the check, and the two started toward the exit just as Alexa and Mark were passing.

Unless they broke into a run or stopped dead in their tracks, they were going to collide with the Whitfields!

Mark stopped, took a handkerchief from his pocket and held it to his face.

Alexa quickly caught on to his maneuver and pretended to help remove something from his eye as Tony and Charlotte started to walk away. As she concentrated on making her ruse effective, Alexa heard Mark curse under his breath and knew they were in trouble.

"They've stopped," he said in a rough whisper.

"They can't recognize us!" It wasn't a question but a cry of hope. She didn't dare turn around.

But she saw the answer in Mark's eyes and then heard it in his voice. "There's something wrong," he said, fixing his well-trained eyes on Charlotte, whom he'd long ago realized was the smarter of the two. "She's being too casual."

"Mark—"

"I want you to get out of here," Mark said, keeping his voice calm. "Try to lose yourself in the crowds, but whatever happens, don't go back to the hotel until you know it's safe." He was counting on Alexa to come through, and Mark's sixth sense told him she could, if only she'd stay in control.

"How, what . . ." Alexa couldn't make herself coherent.

"I'll try to draw them off," Mark said almost brusquely. There wasn't much time now, and he needed Alexa to hurry. "I want you to run. And be careful. Get away. You can do it," he encouraged as he turned and gave her a hefty shove into a group of Japanese tourists, hoping against hope that she would disappear among them.

As Alexa careered through the crowd, Mark began to run in the opposite direction, directly past Charlotte and Tony. Looking back, he could see Tony following him, but his heart sank when Charlotte turned away and pushed through the Japanese. They would slow her down, but would the delay be long enough?

Alexa was clear of the group now and running, remembering the day at the temple of Apollo. Charlotte hadn't climbed; Alexa had. She could only hope that meant she was in a better shape than her pursuer.

At first she increased the distance between them, but had to slow down to avoid a truck that rushed around the corner, almost sideswiping her. With Charlotte gaining on her, Alexa headed down a narrow alley in desperation. Charlotte followed, less than a block away.

Trying to remember all the books she'd read and movies she'd seen where the heroine escaped in a clever feint, Alexa could only visualize car chases along river embankments or up and down San Francisco streets. Swearing at herself for the stupidity of her thoughts, she reached the end of the alley, which opened into a square with an open-air market.

As she crossed the square, a catch in her side almost made her bend double in pain. Gritting her teeth, she ran on. Shoppers stopped to look at her, pointing; dogs barked; and children laughed as she tore by, spurred on by a hidden energy Alexa knew was created from fear.

Through the narrow aisles between stalls she weaved, trying to avoid the baskets piled high with merchandise and succeeding until she reached the last stall. The opening was too narrow, the aisle too crowded for her to pass through without knocking over half the apples and pears that had been stacked in perfect red and yellow rows.

The fruit bounced crazily around, and Alexa almost tripped over it, but kept going even as the proprietor yelled out a stream of Greek curses.

He would have pulled off his apron and run after her if three little boys, seeing fruit available for the taking, hadn't begun to gather it up. Frustrated, the proprietor went after the younger culprits instead.

Charlotte had managed to avoid the melee and was getting closer. Then Alexa saw the bus. It was stopping across the street, taking on the last of a line of passengers. She might be able to make it.

Summoning up one final surge of energy, Alexa sprinted. The door squeaked closed just as she reached it. Desperately she began to pound on it, crying, "*Parakalo, parakalo,* please!" as Charlotte crossed the street and headed toward her.

Alexa cried out again, and almost miraculously the door opened and she fell inside as it closed behind her and the bus lurched away.

Three hours later, when Alexa got back to the hotel, Mark was in the room pacing anxiously. He took her into his arms as soon as she walked through the door.

"Thank heaven," he said as he kissed her deeply, fervently, holding her close.

Alexa clung to him more in exhaustion and relief than in passion. Now that she was safe, her pent-up tension was finally released; her legs grew weak, and she felt herself crumbling in his arms.

Mark swooped her up and took her to the bed where she leaned back against the pillows and closed her eyes. Sitting down beside her, Mark asked, "Where have you been? I was crazy with worry."

Then he noticed that she was wearing a long cotton shift over her tight pants and low-cut blouse. "What in the world is this?" he asked.

"To answer in reverse order," Alexa said, trying to find humor in the situation, "I'm wearing this very proper outfit because I couldn't very well get into the monastery in my Frau Dettwald getup."

"The monastery?"

"Yes," she said with the beginnings of a smile. "In answer to your first question, that's where the bus was going, on a pilgrimage for some obscure saint. So I went along." The smile took over. "You might say that Charlotte missed the bus. What happened to you and Tony?"

Mark didn't answer. He couldn't keep from shaking his head in wonder and admiration. "What a perfect partner in intrigue you are," he said finally, leaning over to kiss her forehead. "I lost Tony, too," he said almost as an afterthought, his lips still grazing her skin.

"What happened?" she asked curiously. "Tell, tell."

Mark laughed. "Just a routine slip, nothing at all exciting. Tony's far less bright and talented than Charlotte. You're amazing, Alexa."

"Want to hire me on your spy team?" she asked jokingly, and then for a moment a sort of sadness came over both of them. Her remark had only served to remind them that their time together was almost over.

Mark gathered her in his arms. "You must be very tired," he said. "There's a long night ahead, Alexa, a dangerous night. I wish you wouldn't—"

"We've already settled this, Mark, and you're not changing my mind. I'm still in it all the way. I just need a little sleep first."

He kissed her again and then lay down beside her, slipping an arm under her shoulders. "Good idea. Take a nap. I'll wake you when it's time for us to leave."

Alexa shivered in the night air and, pushing her hair behind her ears, peered out into the darkness. Moonlight glimmered on the sea. In the distance she could see the dimly lit silhouette of a motor boat drawing near. It was traveling slowly, just barely moving across the surface of the water; the motor hummed softly.

That's the way he'd planned it. As with everything else, Mark had been careful, especially when he'd lifted the key to the boat off the owner after they returned from their trip that afternoon.

Then in the cover of darkness he'd gone to the quay alone, located the boat and let it drift away from the dock before starting the motor. He had time. It never paid to rush. Mark had learned that long ago.

Now as he got closer he could see Alexa wading toward him, keeping the heavy package she was carrying out of the water. She'd done everything so perfectly, and he had no doubt this last, most difficult part of the task would once again find her more than living up to the faith he'd put in her. As he approached her, Mark felt a lump in his throat. She was the closest he'd ever come to happiness.

Mark pulled Alexa into the boat and turned away from shore. "We're on our way," he said, putting aside thoughts of everything but the task ahead of them.

Alexa gave him a thumbs-up signal and sank back on the seat, giving him a tense, anxious smile. This was it. Aphrodite was going home.

They cruised down the coast with Alexa staring into the night, keeping an eye out for landmarks. Everything looked different in the dark—the luminescence of the water, the brilliant flashes of flying fish jumping near the boat, the white curls of waves in the distance. This was Homer's wine-dark sea, and it was as if she and Mark were the only people on it. Alexa looked up at the stars that were clear and bright overhead. It was a lonely night at the end of a long journey.

"There it is," Mark said, and even his voice showed the strain. "The headland."

Alexa squinted into the darkness and saw the delicate columns of the temple of Aphrodite gleaming softly in the moonlight. Behind it, only partially visible, was the mammoth shape of a much older edifice. Deep inside that Mycenaean *tholos* were the bronzes of Hera and Athena, waiting for the return of their sister, the goddess of love.

Everything seemed peaceful and serene until Alexa noticed the jeeps parked near the temple. She'd seen them on their afternoon journey and Mark had told her they belonged to the soldiers on duty. Now, late at night the jeeps were still there, and—somewhere in the area—so were the soldiers.

As a shiver of apprehension ran through her, Alexa reminded herself that this was the only way to get the Aphrodite back where it belonged without the international community finding out the whole story. She and Mark had no other choice, and Alexa had known that when she insisted on coming along.

Now she prepared herself as Mark guided the boat beneath an overhang of the cliff and cut the engine. After dropping anchor, he pulled on his goggles and fins and slipped over the side, treading water easily.

"Hand me the statue," he said, "and then follow me. You saw the cave earlier. It's only a few feet beneath the surface."

Alexa nodded. It had seemed so easy in the daylight with the clear water and colored pebbles visible on the sea floor. Darkness made everything seem sinister, and yet darkness was their cover; it would keep them safe. Or so she hoped.

Alexa secured her goggles and fins and slid into the water.

"The cave is just below us, about half way down," Mark said as he drew a breath and vanished beneath the surface. He'd worried long enough about bringing Alexa along and subjecting her to danger. It was time to go to work with the professionalism that was his trademark and not let her know how desperately he wished she'd stayed behind. It was too late for that. He trusted her, and she would do her best. That was all Mark could ask for.

Alexa said a silent prayer and followed. It was inky black beneath the surface, much darker than she'd imagined. Carrying the extra weight of the statue and supplies, Mark moved swiftly downward, and Alexa had to kick hard to keep up with him. She didn't dare lose sight of Mark and then be left alone in the black, seemingly bottomless sea.

Then she saw it in front of her, the cave opening, a yawning hole. Suddenly she panicked, unable to go in. Childhood fears surfaced, tales of dragons and monsters, sleeping sharks and moray eels all living in dark caverns beneath the sea.

Mark disappeared into the opening, and Alexa knew that if she turned back he would never blame her. It was what he'd wanted all along, and now she feared he might have been right. Holding onto the jutting rock, Alexa stared into the hole. Her lungs were tight and almost bursting; she would have to make a decision in the next few seconds.

Only a few feet above her the boat bobbed on the water, waiting. Below her was the dark unknown, but Mark was there, and that was enough for Alexa. With one strong kick, she pushed into the opening.

It was a totally dark and narrow passage and she was desperate to get through, to break the surface of the water and come up beside Mark. The pressure on her lungs increased until she felt they would explode, and she kicked once more, frantically, before she felt

Mark's hand on her arm, hauling her onto the rocky floor of the cave.

Alexa fell on her back, drawing deep breaths and luxuriating in the chance to get air back into her aching lungs. It wasn't fresh, clean air, but rather fetid and close with a clamminess that seemed to adhere to her. At least it was air, though. At least she could breathe again.

After watching her for an anxious moment, Mark realized she was all right and went to work. First he got his bearings by turning on the flashlight he'd worn clipped to his belt and swinging its beam around the cave.

Alexa sat up as her eyes followed the light. The cave had been carved out of the rock at a time when the sea was higher. Now its walls dripped with rivulets of condensation. It was earth's dark underbelly, and from somewhere in its depths a lizard scurried away from their intrusion. Alexa suppressed a shudder. She didn't like it here, not at all.

Mark shone the flashlight in the corner where the lizard had been lurking behind a pile of debris. When Alexa looked more closely she realized that mixed among the rocks were large shards of pottery.

"They probably date from a much earlier time than the statues," Mark said, swinging the light past the ancient remains until it illuminated the passage. "There it is," he said, helping Alexa to her feet. "I'll show you the way into the *tholos*."

As they moved across the cave he warned her, "You have to bend over here. It's no more than five feet high."

Alexa followed, her shirt and pants damp and dripping, sticking to her skin, but she was grateful for the protection they gave her against the rough rocks. When they reached the shaft, Mark pointed his light into it, and Alexa shook her head in disbelief. "Mark, it's too narrow and steep for anyone to get up."

"There're plenty of footholds in the rock," he said, "and it should still be wide enough for my shoulders."

"Mark, you'll never be able to do it," Alexa said as she stared up into the shaft. "Even with footholds, how in the world—"

"By putting my back against one wall and my feet against the other and inching upward little by little. I've negotiated more difficult climbs than this," he told her, remembering assignments that had seemed impossible but had been managed because of his training. He didn't need to go into that now. It was enough that the problem was easily solvable.

Alexa still looked dubious, so Mark bent over and gave her a quick kiss. "It looks much worse than it is, Alexa, believe me."

Alexa tried to shake off the uncomfortable premonition that she'd had from the moment they'd entered the cave.

"Nothing will happen," he told her again as he positioned himself under the shaft. "I'll go up and drop a line for the statue. All you need to do is attach it and give the rope a pull to let me know it's ready. Piece of cake," he said with a grin.

"Piece of cake," Alexa repeated.

Mark found handholds inside the shaft, and, using the strength of his arms, easily pulled himself up.

Alexa waited below. She could hear a scraping noise and the rasping of his breath as he worked his way bit by bit up the shaft. Then there was silence. Thinking that he'd made it to the top, Alexa held on to the statue, waiting patiently for him to drop the rope.

Long minutes passed, and she heard nothing. Finally she could stand the suspense no longer and called out softly, "Mark, what's happened? Mark...?"

Then she heard him again, this time moving back down the shaft toward her. First his long legs appeared, and then he dropped to the ground beside Alexa, uttering a curse under his breath.

"What is it?" she asked nervously.

"I can't get through," he answered. "There's no way."

"But I thought—"

"It was my mistake," he admitted, "not to have checked it out earlier, but I just assumed—" He broke off. "I reached a spot where my shoulders couldn't get through, no matter how I maneuvered. The rocks have shifted," he told her, "and there's no way I can move them." Mark obviously couldn't believe that he'd made such a mistake, and for a moment he even wondered if he could be losing his touch. In frustration, he pounded his fist into the palm of his other hand, swearing under his breath.

"I can do it," Alexa said.

At first he didn't seem to hear her, and then when he realized what she was offering, he looked down at her in astonishment.

"My shoulders are smaller than yours. I can get through," Alexa said with a calmness she didn't feel.

Mark continued to stare at her, shaking his head. "No way. I'm not asking you to do this."

"You're not asking, Mark," she reminded him. "I'm volunteering."

A thousand objections went through his brain, but he voiced the most obvious one. "What about your fear of heights?"

"That's only when I climb rickety old ladders. Remember that I went up the cliffs to the temple of Apollo like a mountain goat. I can do it," she said with a firmness that actually gave her courage.

"You don't have to. You know that, Alexa."

She heard the hope mixed with the anxiety in his voice. "We don't have time for a long discussion, Mark. Let's get going," she said briskly.

Mark's answer was to pull her close and kiss her. His arms were strong, and his mouth was warm and comforting on hers. He gave her courage and sustenance. More than anything, she didn't want to let him down.

"I can't let you go," he said, holding her closer.

"There's no other way," Alexa said logically. "Let's just hope I can do the job when I get up there."

"You can," he assured her. "Sir William guaranteed that the switch would be easy. Apparently the statues fit into a slot on the marble base. All you have to do is pull the fake one out and replace it with our Aphrodite."

"Piece of cake," she said with a grin.

"No, Alexa," he told her, "it's not that simple."

"You said before—"

"It's different for me," he told her.

"Aren't you applying a double standard, Mark?"

He put his hands on her shoulders and looked down at her. "You know better. I don't think like that, but the simple fact is, I've had years of experience, and you're—"

"A beginner," she finished for him. "But I've had a good teacher, and I'm ready. If you'll just give me a leg up."

Mark knew that he had no other choice if he wanted to replace the statue. His training told him he was making a mistake, his instinct told him he wasn't. Mark decided to follow his instinct.

Trying to ignore his desire to take Alexa in his arms and keep her there with him, Mark leaned over, patted her affectionately on the bottom and started to boost her into the shaft.

"Wait," she said suddenly. "What if the top of the *tholos* is blocked? I imagine it's been covered for years."

"You're right," Mark said, pleased that her thought processes were so in tune with his. "I checked with Sir William, and he assured me that somehow he'd arrange accessibility to the opening. We have to count on his having done that."

"Then that's it," Alexa said. "I'm ready."

Without another word, Mark heaved her up until she was inside the shaft.

"Ugh," she said, wrinkling her nose, "it smells terrible." She tried not to think about the centipedes and spiders that were certainly lurking in the slimy crevasses of the rocks.

Mark gave her one more push and Alexa was on her own. Following his instructions, she pressed her back into one wall and braced her feet against the other, bending her knees. Little by little, using her feet and hands, she began to climb.

At first it was easy. Then the shaft narrowed and progress became slow and painful. Alexa's legs began to ache; her muscles trembled. She could feel the sweat running down her face and back, and she wanted desperately to stop and rest.

But there was no way to relax with the constant pressure on her legs and back just to keep herself from falling. She had no choice but to go on.

She wished that she could see light from the *tholos*, something that would give her the will to keep on. But there was no light. Alexa would have to find the will within herself.

She shifted her weight, took a deep breath and pushed her back against the wall, but when she tried to move her legs, one foot slipped. Alexa reached out to catch herself, dislodging a rock from the shaft. She could hear it falling, ricocheting against the sides of the wall.

Mark heard the rock dropping, and even though he knew better than to call out, he had to know she was all right. "Alexa," he cried, "Alexa!"

She was the one who made the right decision then. She knew better than to respond. One of the guards might be close enough to hear. So she remained silent, scrambling for a hold and managing to steady herself. She would make it, Alexa told herself; the fatigue had passed, and she'd gotten a second wind. Even the muscles in her legs seemed less tight now.

Then she realized that it wasn't height she feared but dark, confined places. As she worked her way upward Alexa tried desperately to fight the claustrophobia that was taking over, but each time she inched forward it swept through her again, and soon she'd broken into a cold, clammy sweat.

Then she thought about Mark, waiting for her, trusting her, and she tried to move on as if he were with her. The fear of reaching out and touching a snake or some feral, dark creature, the fear that she would somehow get lodged in the narrow tunnel and never escape, all the fears that she'd experienced during her climb surfaced one by one, and she fought them off by imagining he was beside her.

After that it was easy. The cramps in her legs, the scrapes on her hands as she clawed for holds in the rock, the pain in her back were ignored as she moved upward with a surge.

All at once her momentum was halted. She'd hit something. She could go no further. At first, Alexa thought her way was blocked, then she realized that she was at her goal. She'd reached the top.

She pushed against the obstacle that covered the opening. It felt like a wooden cover, but it wasn't heavy, and with a little effort she was able to move it aside and look out, feeling the cool air on her face.

She'd expected it to be dark, but there was a light in the *tholos* that caused her to duck back down quickly, holding her breath, waiting for a guard to call out.

There was only silence.

Slowly she emerged again. The light was faint, but she could see well enough to tell that she was alone in a room filled with artifacts and carved statuary. Alexa didn't stop to examine the works of art; there wasn't time. Besides, she'd found what she was looking for.

The gate was by far the most spectacular piece in the room. In awe Alexa approached the masterpiece with the bronze statues of Athena and Hera, and in the center the golden Aphrodite. The copy was good, Alexa had to admit, but it couldn't compare to the original.

Reaching up, she carefully removed the Aphrodite from its marble base. Then she stood absolutely still for a long moment, hoping no one heard the noise. Satisfied with the silence, Alexa moved swiftly but quietly back to the shaft and lowered the weighted rope to Mark.

She felt the slack when it hit bottom, followed by a sharp tug which meant Mark was ready, and she began to pull the real statue up the shaft. Hand over hand she pulled the heavy canvas case, trying to ignore the rope burns on her palms, pulling with all her strength.

Then she heard a voice calling out. She froze, her feet braced, her arms tense, holding the rope so it wouldn't slip through her hands.

Perspiration poured down her forehead as Alexa waited. According to Sir William, the guards only patrolled the area in front of the *tholos*. But any suspicious noise would certainly bring them running. Alexa strained to hear the soldier's words and then let out a sigh of relief as she translated the Greek. He hadn't called out a warning at all, only a request for a cigarette!

Feeling safe, Alexa gave the rope one more pull and was able to reach down and grab the handles of the canvas bag. She opened it up, took out the real statue and replaced it with the fake. Her job was almost done, but Alexa didn't think she had the strength left in her hands to lower the canvas bag. Instead she let the rope drop through the shaft and pushed the bag after it.

Then she moved stealthily across the room and put the real Aphrodite in its rightful place. It was over; she'd done what she and Mark had set out to do days ago. She turned to leave and then stopped, touching the statue lovingly on its golden cheek. "Welcome home, Aphrodite."

Going down the shaft was much easier, but it still seemed like a long, dark eternity before she reached the bottom and fell into Mark's arms. Cradled against him, Alexa felt that she, too, had come home. She didn't think of the future, only of now. "We did it, Mark," she said.

"*You* did it, Alexa," he answered, "and I've never been as proud of anyone in my life, even though you almost crowned me with the fake statue when you dropped it down the shaft."

Alexa laughed wearily. "I didn't have an ounce of energy left," she told him, "so I just had to hope you'd move out of the way."

"Fortunately I had an idea that was your plan when I saw the rope coming at me," he said with a laugh. "You're some woman, Alexa." He gave her a fierce hug. "Now let's get the hell out of here."

Chapter 12

Alexa woke up slowly, pushing away layer after layer of sleep. Her first waking sensation came from the bright sunlight flooding the room, followed by an unexpected ache in her bones. Then she remembered. They'd fallen into bed after returning to the hotel at sunrise.

Without turning over, she could sense the comfortable warmth of Mark's body next to hers, and if she listened carefully, Alexa could hear the faint sound of his breathing. She smiled to herself. He'd always been a quiet sleeper.

Always. Alexa closed her eyes and tried not to face what had to be faced. Always was over. Today was their last day.

Very quietly, so that she wouldn't waken him, Alexa turned to look at Mark. In sleep he seemed younger and much more vulnerable, not at all the tough, competent man who'd shared so many adventures with her and who'd spent most of his adult life in the secret service performing duties far more dangerous.

That man was very little in evidence beside her. Instead, she saw his boyish side, the Mark that had surfaced often in their time together. In fact, that was the only Mark she'd known until she had learned who he really was and their trip with Aphrodite had begun.

He stirred slightly and opened his eyes, smiling when he saw her watching him. "*Kalimera*, Alexa," he said, and for a wonderful moment time rushed backward and she saw him standing in the road beside her house, his knapsack slung over his shoulder.

"*Kalimera*, Marco."

"How're you feeling?" His eyes were solicitous as he rolled onto his side so that he could look up at her. "Are you okay?" One hand reached out to caress her arm and shoulder.

"A little stiff and sore," she admitted, "but nothing that a good breakfast won't cure."

"More like lunch," he commented, looking at the light pouring in through the window and then at his watch. "It's almost noon."

"Really?" Alexa couldn't remember when she'd last slept so late.

"Of course, it was nearly dawn when we got to bed," Mark reminded her. He moved his fingers down her arm to her hand and turned it so that he could see the palm. It was red and scratched. "Poor darling," he said, giving her a kiss.

"My hands are a mess," Alexa admitted.

"Badges of honor," Mark corrected her, kissing her palm again before moving his lips to caress each of her fingers with infinite care, one by one.

As his mouth lingered, he glanced up at her, and their eyes locked in a long, hungry look. Everything was quiet and still; even the noises from outside seemed muted.

The sunlight illuminated them with a fierce, unearthly glow. Alexa could see the slow rise and fall of Mark's chest and feel the heat of his eyes devouring her. He reached out and stroked her face, and his touch was so gentle, so sensitive, that Alexa closed her eyes, luxuriating in the feeling brought on by his care and concern.

Yet it was a feeling much more than that, and Alexa knew it. Between them was an understanding that she knew she'd never experience again. She wanted to capture the moment and keep it with her forever.

Mark moved his hand upward to her neck, tracing slow, sensual patterns against her skin. Alexa sighed and opened her eyes, looking at him, loving him.

He smiled in return and leaned over to kiss her lips before moving his hand lower and cupping her breasts with wonderful sensitivity and longing. Her nipples tautened at his touch, and Mark used the palm of his hand to rub and tease and tantalize her through the soft cotton gown.

Deep within Alexa, a warmth began to flicker and flare. It was as penetrating as the sunlight that bathed them in a golden glow, as hot and insistent as the rays that beat down on them. In fact, she didn't even feel the sun, but the glow inside her couldn't be denied.

"Oh, Alexa," she heard him say, "my Alexa."

Without another word, he slipped the gown over her head and tossed it onto the floor so that she lay nude before his eyes, her sunshine-dappled body luminous and glowing.

Mark moved his hands down her body, across her hips to her thighs, loving her just as his lips and eyes loved her. Alexa reacted to every move, every touch, every look, melting inside, hungry for more.

He kissed the hollow between her breasts and then the pink bud of her nipple, and the warmth that had been as pervasive as the sun's rays spread and flamed within her.

She could hear the quickening of Mark's breath, feel its sweetness on her breast and then on her abdomen and at the curve of her waist. His touch was exquisite. His tongue traced the line of her hip and glided along her thigh.

Longing for fulfillment even as she reveled in the tortuous ascent toward it, Alexa reached for him, her hands greedily sliding over the smooth, damp muscles of his back, across the hard, flat planes of his stomach to the rising thrust of his desire.

She touched him as he'd touched her, first with gentle fingers and then with loving kisses. He lay back, eyes closed, lost in his passion and pleasure.

All Alexa could think of was Mark. He filled her heart as he filled her soul. She was touching him, kissing him, loving him for the last time, and she wanted it to go on forever even though she knew it was near the end.

Slowly he lifted her until she was above him, and with his hands guiding her, holding her, Alexa slid down upon his arousal, and he filled her utterly and completely, in every way. He filled all the emptiness of her body just as he filled the corners of her life.

As their eyes met once more, their joining seemed as spiritual as it was physical. Two beings with but one body, complete, each becoming part of the other by giving and receiving pleasure, endlessly.

They moved together with a oneness that seemed like a kind of miracle, and yet it was so very, very real. Alexa could feel every pleasurable thrust as she moved upon him, every deep, thrilling penetration of her body. And with each, the passion and desire spiraled through her until she thought she could bear no more.

Her body reacted to the ecstasy and longed for it to go on and on even as Alexa knew it had to end and that the end would be the ultimate pleasure. Still, she wanted to delay it.

As Mark moved with her, he also seemed to be holding back, prolonging the moment. With his hands around her waist, he lifted Alexa until they were almost separated and held her there for an endless moment of agonizing pleasure until neither of them could wait any longer. Then he eased her back down and this final time filled her so completely that her breath caught in her throat.

In order to be sure that she hadn't stopped breathing, Alexa called out, and the word on her lips was his name. "Mark, Mark!" It was the only sound in the room, the only proof that they were still of this world and not catapulted somewhere out into the darkness of infinity.

Then for one brief moment they *were* in another world, hearing only the echo of her voice calling his name through endless time and space as their release swept away everything but their passion, glowing white-hot in the sun.

Mark rolled her over until they were side by side, with their bodies still joined. Moving his hands over her, he looked into her eyes with a feeling of such intensity that Alexa found herself saying, "I love you, Mark. I love you."

"And I love you, Alexa," he responded, "more than you can imagine."

Mark covered her with his body, and she felt his weight bringing her back to a moment in time that she'd almost lost. She wished that she had lost it as she waited in vain for him to say more, to talk of their future. But there was only Mark and the weight of his body.

So Alexa forced herself to stay in the moment and the little that she had left of him. His heaviness on her was damp and hot and she cherished it and drifted back into a half sleep beneath him, holding on to all that was left.

Later, as they dressed, Alexa was still holding on to time but trying not to show her sadness. When he suggested they go down to the harbor for lunch, she agreed with a smile.

"We still have a couple of hours before the ceremony, so let's enjoy them as tourists."

"What about Tony and Charlotte?" Alexa asked.

Mark shrugged. "I imagine they'll still be hot on the trail of the golden Aphrodite until she's unveiled at the ceremony today."

"So they'll still be after us," Alexa said.

"No doubt. But it doesn't matter, does it? Maybe if we see them we can invite them over to our table for an ouzo," he teased.

Alexa laughed. They were safe, and suddenly she was anxious to be out of the room, away from the intimacy of the rumpled bed. "Let's go," she said cheerily. Her future with Mark extended only to the ceremony that afternoon, no further. It was time to begin putting space between them.

They didn't talk very much at lunch. The separation had already begun, and with it had come a loss of intimacy, a politeness that Alexa contributed to as much as Mark did. It had to be.

When it was finally time to leave for the hotel, they walked along the quay, both very quiet, lost in their own thoughts.

Alexa was surprised when Mark took her hand and said very casually, "Tony's behind us."

She kept walking, not breaking stride. "Hard to avoid them, I guess, in a town with one main street," she said. "Has he seen us?"

"Sure has," Mark said.

"What should we do?"

"Nothing—*or* we could really give him something to look at." He pulled her close, kissing her thoroughly and completely to the delight of the shop owners and passersby. "Let's let him think we're so lost in each other that we don't even know he exists," Mark said, kissing her again.

Tears filled Alexa's eyes, for she *was* lost, lost in love with Mark. But for him, she knew, it was still an assignment—not even an assignment, really, just a game.

When they reached the hotel, Mark looked over his shoulder and murmured, "Tony's discreetly lingering across the street. I'm sure as soon as we leave he'll be in our room like a shark on a kill."

This time he kissed her lightly on the cheek. "I'll get the car. We wouldn't want to be late for the ceremony."

Mark and Alexa stood in the hot sun along with the high-ranking dignitaries, special guests and members of the international press as Sir William officially returned the Aphrodite gate to the Greek minister of culture.

Sir William's speech was moving and eloquent, and Alexa wasn't the only one to feel tears sting her eyes.

"Aphrodite has come home," Sir William said, echoing in public what Alexa had spoken in private just a few hours before. She couldn't help smiling to herself as she thought of the real story of Aphrodite's travels.

"We of the British Museum," Sir William went on, "are pleased to return her and her sister goddesses to the sunshine of Greece."

The ceremony was held only a few yards from the *tholos* at the ruins of Aphrodite's temple. The three goddesses had comprised a portion of the temple's once-spectacular gate. Now they were all that was left, set in place among the remaining sections of the temple—the slender columns and massive foundation that was another of many testimonies to what had once been the splendor of Greece. What remained intact was the natural beauty of the scenery, the massive cliffs, the azure sea and above, the clear blue of a sky found nowhere else in the world.

"This place," Sir William continued with a wide sweep of his hands to encompass it all, "this wonderful land of Greece has seen so much: the birth of civilization, art and architecture and literature, and for all of those gifts we are forever grateful.

"But this land has also seen tragedy and bloodshed. We are pleased to be able to wipe away some of that stain by returning this magnificent gate to its home." He paused a moment to let his words sink in. "Therefore, in the name of Her Majesty and all the citizens of Great Britain, I return to the Temple of Aphrodite its most treasured artifact."

He stepped forward and pulled away the cloth that covered the gate. Aphrodite gleamed in the Greek sunlight with a new radiance, with Hera and Athena on either side. Once more, Alexa felt the sting of tears in her eyes as a gasp of delight rippled through the crowd, followed by a surge of applause. It was over.

Now there was nothing left for Alexa but to retrace her steps, hopefully more speedily and less adventurously this time, and return home to Kavos. Not, however, until she met Sir William.

He was exactly as Alexa had always pictured him, tall and distinguished with white hair and mustache, the typical English scholar and gentleman. But to Mark, Alexa knew, he was much more.

"He wants to thank you personally," Mark told her after the crowd had thinned out. They approached Sir William, who grasped Alexa's hand in a firm and warm greeting.

"My dear Miss Cord, how pleased I am to meet you after all my godson has told me." Alexa believed she saw him wink, which seemed terribly unscholarly but somehow very appropriate. Naturally he couldn't speak of what she and Mark had done except in the most veiled terms.

"As I'm sure you know, all of us at the museum will be eternally grateful to you for sharing our concern that this beautiful gate be returned to Greece intact, and we want to thank you particularly for your efforts on our behalf."

"I am happy that I could help," Alexa said, "for the sake of my grandfather and my family."

"Of course, of course," Sir William said, understanding more than anyone who overheard the conversation could have suspected. "Now let us all have a drink together, please, before we go our separate ways, too soon, I am afraid."

Alexa agreed, uncertain just how much time was left. Mark hadn't told her; obviously he'd thought it better that way, but it came as a shock when Sir William looked at his watch and said, "Then I had best call the car to take you to your plane, dear boy."

"Yes, it's about that time," Mark agreed.

"You're packed?"

Mark nodded. "The driver is stopping for my bag on the way here."

Alexa had listened to their words, not really understanding at first. When it hit her that Mark was leaving immediately, she looked up at him with a terrible sadness in her eyes.

He answered the unspoken question. "It seems my superiors want me back as soon as possible."

Sir William, unaware of the distress that Alexa was fighting to control, explained further. "Mark has been on a sort of sabbatical with this little assignment, and the powers that be have what they consider more important work for him to do. It is imminent, I believe, as everything from that department seems always to be," he added with a touch of humor.

"We're all expendable, Sir William, but they like to think the world can't do without our department."

Obviously the "department" was code for the British secret service. Whatever it was, Alexa didn't really care. She only knew that Mark was leaving without even time for a real goodbye.

"As for you, my dear," Sir William was saying, "I've arranged for a private plane to fly you back to Rhodes this evening, if that is convenient for you. From there, I believe, you can take a ferry to your island."

"Yes," Alexa murmured and then remembered her manners. "That's very kind of you, Sir William. I wondered how I was going to get home." Somehow the word "home" had less of a golden ring to it than in the past. Kavos was her home now, but it would be very different without Mark.

"My dear, it is the least we can do after all that you've done for us. And I believe I do owe you some explanation of what has happened."

At first Alexa thought the older man was talking about Mark and his untimely leave-taking, but he had something else in mind.

"We are completely safe here, are we not, Mark?"

"Completely," Mark said.

The threesome was at a table on the wharf with no one nearby but the sea gulls that were perched on the railing and on the mast of a sailboat in the harbor.

"Apparently a woman in my employ at the British Museum has been acting as a—what do you call it, Mark?"

"A mole, Sir William."

"Ah, yes, somewhat depressing term, it seems to me but in any case the woman is connected with an unfriendly government prepared to go to any lengths to embarrass Great Britain in the international community."

"Charlotte Whitfield," Alexa said. "Mark told me she was involved, but I thought it was for personal gain."

"That was our first suspicion," Mark told her. "Apparently it's more far-reaching."

Sir William nodded. "Far-reaching enough to interest Mark's people."

"What about Tony?" Alexa asked.

"No more than a rich playboy," Mark answered, "whom Charlotte brought into her little adventure. As I suspected, hardly the brains of the duo."

"Then they aren't brother and sister. I certainly am gullible," Alexa said.

"It takes years of training to spot these kinds of operators," Mark told her.

"What's going to happen to them?" Alexa wondered.

"You'll have to ask Mark and his people about that," was Sir William's response.

Mark shrugged. "We'll let them sail around for a while and see what other mischief they're up to.

Charlotte's not a very big prize, but she may have some information we can use. In any case, she's a trained operative and possibly even dangerous, but she was no match for Alexa, Sir William," Mark added.

"I'm not surprised. Alexa is very special. Now, Mark," Sir William said, changing the subject abruptly, "We will have to bid you farewell. It's time."

"Yes," Mark answered.

"Shall I take our rental car back to the hotel?" Alexa asked in a voice that surprised her with its calmness.

"That's a good idea," Mark said. "I'll walk you to the car before I leave," he added.

"And I'll see you later this evening, dear girl," Sir William added, shaking Alexa's hand energetically. "I'll tell your driver to wait," he called after Mark and Alexa.

They stood by the rental car, avoiding each other's eyes for a long moment before Alexa spoke. "You're going to be late, Mark."

"Alexa, I—"

"You don't have to explain. I understand," she said.

But he tried to explain anyway, as if that would help. "I knew I would have to go back today, but I didn't want that to spoil anything for us."

"I understand," she repeated, and they both knew that she didn't. Suddenly the air was very still and unbearably hot. The sunlight that had bathed them in its splendor earlier was now hazy and heavy. In the heat of the afternoon, the street was almost deserted.

"I knew this would happen, our saying goodbye," she told him. "I knew the day you appeared at my gate with the Help Wanted sign." It was true; her mind had known, but not her heart. Somehow her heart couldn't believe even now that it would end. "It doesn't matter how or when it happens."

"But it does," Mark protested. "I know it does, and yet there's no way I could have avoided this." His face looked tired and strained, and for the first time Alexa realized that their goodbye was as difficult for him as for her.

"You have Kavos and the inn," he said.

"Yes, I'm more determined than ever to make a go of it, and you've given me a good start." The silence that hung between them seemed to engulf the whole quay. No sound was heard, no movement made.

"And you'll go back to your real job," she added finally, admitting at last that he was leaving.

"Yes, my holiday's over."

"Some holiday," she ventured.

He took her by the shoulders and held her at arm's length. "A wonderful holiday. I met you."

Alexa tried to move away, but he wouldn't let her. "I meant everything I said, Alexa. I'm just sorry that the timing was wrong for us."

She turned away and looked out to the harbor. "You left some things at the house. A few books. Some clothes."

"Keep them for me. Who knows? Maybe some day I'll spend another holiday on Kavos."

Alexa waited for him to open the car door, and when he seemed reluctant to make that final move, she opened it herself and got in. She felt her lip begin to quiver, but turned it into a smile as she looked up at him. "Goodbye, Mark," she said brightly, determined not to cry, at least not in front of him. "Take care."

"You, too, Alexa. I'll never forget you."

Somehow she managed to fight off the tears until she rounded the corner out of his sight.

Mark watched her drive off and then walked back to the street where Sir William waited. Before nightfall, he'd be in England again. Somehow the thought did nothing to lift his spirits.

Sir William held out his hand as Mark approached. "I expect I'll see you in a few days' time," he said. "For dinner at the club, perhaps."

"Yes," Mark responded. His eyes were still following the route of Alexa's car, now far out of sight.

Sir William, noticing Mark's preoccupation, said, "I could have arranged for her to accompany you to the airport."

Mark's driver opened the car door for him, and Mark got in, answering his godfather, "No, that would just have prolonged things. It was better this way. Short and sweet."

Sir William leaned over as the driver started up the engine. "But that doesn't make it any easier, does it?"

"It's never easy to say goodbye to the woman you love."

Epilogue

It was a glorious autumn day on Kavos. The sky was an incredible October blue, and the air was still warm and balmy, the fall flowers more colorful than they'd been in years. Or so the villagers told her. Alexa hardly had time to notice.

She'd managed to finish three rooms at the Villa Alexi and by late summer had taken in her first guest. Now there were four tourists sitting at the tables in the garden, dawdling over their coffee.

Alexa had refilled their cups and was just returning to the house when she heard the gate open. She still hadn't gotten around to fixing the latch, and friends and relatives always ignored the brass knocker and came on in.

Expecting that Sophie had walked up the hill to share a cup of coffee and bask in the success of Villa Alexi, she didn't even bother to look up but headed into the kitchen, returned the pot to the stove, sat down at the table and prepared herself for the morning gossip.

When the expected greeting from her great aunt wasn't forthcoming, Alexa finally glanced toward the door. There was no one to be seen.

"Sophie," she called out.

Getting no answer, Alexa rose from the table, a little exasperated, and went out into the courtyard. Sometimes the tourists came in without knocking and then became confused about where to go next. It was still more like a home than an inn, and Alexa liked it that way.

"Come on in," she called out as she walked into the courtyard.

She saw the shadow move across the cobblestones before she realized that he was standing right in front of her, blond and bearded and handsome as ever.

"Mark..." The rest of the sentence froze in her throat.

He wanted to reach out and take her in his arms, but he didn't dare. He held her with his eyes instead, commenting on the house as if he'd been there only the day before, as if their conversation was simply taking up where it'd left off. In a way, it was.

"I like what you've done," he said. "The villa looks just the way I expected."

"I've gotten a great deal accomplished," Alexa said, her newfound voice a little shaky.

He saw her nervousness, but it was no greater than his own.

"I can tell," he answered.

"The reward from the British Museum helped considerably, but I guess you know all about that."

"Sir William mentioned it. I understand you have a few guests."

"Four, in fact."

"The judicious marketing campaign worked, I see."

"It's beginning to. That, and some well-placed advertising. So far my income is far below the promotional costs." Her words sounded strained and stilted. This wasn't at all what she wanted to say. She wanted to reach out for him and touch him, but she held back, unsure.

"That's to be expected," Mark said. He hadn't taken his eyes off her and wasn't even aware of what they were saying to each other. He only knew that she was there, filling his eyes and his heart. So near and yet so far away.

"Yes," she agreed. "As soon as word of mouth takes over..." She didn't have the energy to say anything else. She was exhausted emotionally, and the words just wouldn't come. Leaning back against the door, she noticed for the first time that he was holding one of her Help Wanted flyers.

"Some things haven't changed," she managed to say.

"So I see." A smile curled his lips. "Handymen are always hard to come by. As you may remember, I've had a little experience."

"Honed your plumbing and electrical skills?"

"Yes, and some tile work and roofing as well."

"Sounds good, but I'll be needing someone full-time, and I understand you have another job." Alexa struggled to get her breath as she waited for his response.

"Not any longer," Mark told her. "I resigned."

Alexa felt her heart pounding. "Oh? I thought that was nearly impossible in your field."

"I'm one of the lucky ones. Managed to phase out of the service with a substantial retirement fund."

"Won't you miss the work?" she asked. It had been his life for so long, and Alexa had finally convinced herself that it always would be. Now he was here, standing before her, and she wanted to know, she *had* to know.

"Alexa, it *was* the life for me, you're absolutely right. For years I thought I never would find anything to replace it, but I was wrong. I found you."

Her heartbeat returned to normal, and Alexa managed to catch her breath, finally. In the garden, she could hear her guests getting up, moving away toward the hills for a walk after breakfast. She silently thanked them for leaving her alone with Mark.

"As I mentioned, the retirement is more than adequate, and I'm looking for a good investment . . . and a partner," he said.

"I just happen to own an inn on one of the most beautiful of the Greek islands. It's operating in the red at the moment."

"But there's great potential for profit," he observed. "That takes care of the investment part. Now, about the partner." He smiled down at her. "I think this should be a lifetime arrangement."

With a sigh, Alexa stepped into his outstretched arms. "I believe that can be arranged," she said as his lips captured hers.

Across the courtyard came the sound of the brass knocker. Two more guests had arrived, but it would take a few minutes before they realized that the latch was rusted and the door would swing open on its own. By that time, Mark and Alexa would have walked across the courtyard to greet them and welcome them to Villa Alexi.

*   *   *   *   *

Silhouette Special Edition.

presents

★ LOVE AND GLORY ★

from
Lindsay McKenna

Introducing a gripping new series celebrating our men—and women—in uniform. Meet the Trayherns, a military family as proud and colorful as the American flag, a family fighting the shadow of dishonor, a family determined to triumph—with **LOVE AND GLORY!**

June: **A QUESTION OF HONOR** (SE #529) leads the fast-paced excitement. When Coast Guard officer Noah Trayhern offers Kit Anderson a safe house, he unwittingly endangers his own guarded emotions.

July: **NO SURRENDER** (SE #535) Navy pilot Alyssa Trayhern's assignment with arrogant jet jockey Clay Cantrell threatens her career—and her heart—with a crash landing!

August: **RETURN OF A HERO** (SE #541) Strike up the band to welcome home a man whose top-secret reappearance will make headline news . . . with a delicate, daring woman by his side.

Three courageous siblings—
three consecutive months of

★ LOVE AND GLORY ★

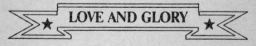

Premiering in **June**, only in
Silhouette Special Edition.

FOUR UNIQUE SERIES
FOR EVERY WOMAN YOU ARE...

Silhouette Romance

Love, at its most tender, provocative, emotional... in stories that will make you laugh and cry while bringing you the magic of falling in love.

6 titles per month

Silhouette Special Edition

Sophisticated, substantial and packed with emotion, these powerful novels of life and love will capture your imagination and steal your heart.

6 titles per month

Silhouette Desire

Open the door to romance and passion. Humorous, emotional, compelling—yet always a believable and sensuous story—Silhouette Desire never fails to deliver on the promise of love.

6 titles per month

Silhouette Intimate Moments

Enter a world of excitement, of romance heightened by suspense, adventure and the passions every woman dreams of. Let us sweep you away.

4 titles per month

SILG-1R

You'll flip . . . your pages won't!
Read paperbacks *hands-free* with

Book Mate • I

The perfect "mate" for all your romance paperbacks

Traveling • Vacationing • At Work • In Bed • Studying • Cooking • Eating

Perfect size for all standard paperbacks, this wonderful invention makes reading a pure pleasure! Ingenious design holds paperback books OPEN and FLAT so even wind can't ruffle pages — leaves your hands free to do other things. Reinforced, wipe-clean vinyl-covered holder flexes to let you turn pages without undoing the strap . . . supports paperbacks so well, they have the strength of hardcovers!

Pages turn WITHOUT opening the strap.

SEE-THROUGH STRAP

Reinforced back stays flat.

Built in bookmark

BOOK MARK

BACK COVER HOLDING STRIP

10˝ x 7¼˝ opened.
Snaps closed for easy carrying, too

Available now. Send your name, address, and zip code, along with a check or money order for just $5.95 + .75¢ for postage & handling (for a total of $6.70) payable to Reader Service to:

Reader Service
Bookmate Offer
901 Fuhrmann Blvd.
P.O. Box 1396
Buffalo, N.Y. 14269-1396

Offer not available in Canada
*New York and Iowa residents add appropriate sales tax.

BM-G

Silhouette Intimate Moments™

COMING NEXT MONTH

#289 TIGER DAWN—Kathleen Creighton

Zoologist Sarah Fairchild was one of the privileged, the elite, and Dan Cisco knew that his kind and hers didn't mix. But when poachers threatened Sarah and her orangutans he realized that society's rules could always be broken in the name of love.

#290 THE PRICE OF GLORY—
Lynn Bartlett

It was déjà vu for news bureau chief Seth Winter. Once terrorists had taken the lives of his wife and child; now they had kidnapped his star reporter, Cassandra Blake, the woman who had brought love back into his life. This time, he swore, justice—and the heart—would triumph.

#291 ABOVE SUSPICION—
Andrea Edwards

Trapped in a web of danger and deceit, Claire Haywood knew that only love could set her free. But if she told Jonathon Tyler the truth and admitted that she'd begun their relationship as a spy, would he be able to see the genuine love beneath the lies?

#292 LIAR'S MOON—Mary Anne Wilson

Michael Conti was a finder of missing people, and during his most recent assignment he'd discovered the love of his life. But his findings also suggested that Alexandria Thomas was a thief. And it was true—because he knew she'd stolen his heart.
